ONIONS BUNIONS CORNS AND DUNGEONS

D.D. CROSS

Novels by D.D. Cross

A Den of Brigands

Forheavenstake

Field of Corns

Heapatrouble

Back to Hades: Eustice Seeney Returns to Hell

Go to Hell! (I DID) Interview With Eustice Seeney

Devilzinthedetails

Hellitatinteasy

ONIONS BUNIONS CORNS AND DUNGEONS

D.D. Cross

MMA

Publishing

D.D. CROSS

ONIONS BUNIONS CORNS AND DUNGEONS

A truth that's told with bad intent beats all the lies you can invent.
~William Blake

Time is not an obstacle, it's something we all have to pass through unless we get dead on the way.
~Eddy Mexico

Abe Lincoln's Double O Seven

Dr. Issachar Zacharie (1827-1900 or so they say) was more than Abraham Lincoln's chiropodist, the British New Yorker was a confidant who whilst removing President Lincoln's troublesome corns made his way into the secrets of the Confederacy during the US Civil War. The good doctor was America's first James Bond, and Herman Duss wanted to be just like that.

Who was Herman Duss?

D.D. CROSS

1

The fabric of reality--that which exists, even if you don't believe in it--is woven from threads, fibers, filaments, and strands on a loom made from elements outside of human comprehension.

Within this reality is the tapestry of human history, a weave of patterns governed by the materials that make up the cloth: laws of the physical universe, and human physiology.

A recurring theme since man's emergence from the cave is a quest for more than what life had to offer. With each generation there are people in search of some treatment, tonic, potion, or venture to alter their destiny. Another set of humans accompany the seekers with similar enthusiasm, but their motives are exploitative, dubious, and often self-serving. The cloth of history is stained by charlatans, quacks, hucksters, and frauds who've woven their way into the texture of time.

A constant theme throughout has been that some supernatural, mystical, magical items, practices, or phenomena of profound transformative nature existed in some form or another. Some believed they could harness these "powers," and enhance the state of humanity, or destroy it.

Widely held beliefs, clues to some of the great secrets were hidden among the ruins of lost civilizations: from Anubis Gates, the Pyramids, Treasures of King Solomon's Mines, the Lost Continent of Atlantis, Easter Island's glyphs, Nazca Lines, UFO landing strips, Stonehenge, the Bermuda Triangle, chiropractors, the foreskin of Jesus Christ, naturopaths, faith healers, and practitioners of dubious intent, selling supplements that have made for some of the most colorful urine and feces in history. The list goes on.

Throughout history many items of the occult were hidden to prevent them from falling into the hands of incapable, ignorant, uninitiated, or worse: an enemy who might use these powers against you. Secret societies spotted the curtains and currents of bygone times. Some trinkets were secreted away by other tribes, nations, or armies. Whispers of conspiracies went unheard, but the shroud of mystery remained.

There were in all times tightly held beliefs that somehow this "magic" could have saved some poor soul from a miserable end, but that's life. Right?

The fact that no one had a clue what these recurring items of the occult could really do persisted for centuries, and often they were surrounded by some curse, hex, warning or fear. Suffering, disappearance, unexplained deaths, theories, volumes of research, folklore, and just plain bullshit.

A substance found at nearly all of the human places on earth where the bizarre, curious, undetermined, unknowns exist. It's a common substance, thought at first to be of no earthly origin. Those thoughts were incorrect.

The commonality was this: a crystal of sorts existed at each locale either incorporated into some other item as a liquid, solid, or gas, but remained in its ubiquity for no earthly reason. This form of crystal had no place among earth's periodic table of the elements, or any category at all. The fact that it existed and couldn't be explained, yet had a unique albeit frightening effect on those who came in contact with it. It mesmerized, hypnotized, terrified, and mortified the hordes. A need to know subculture grew, and despite adversity its capabilities were discovered. The substance was isolated in 2040, and mankind became capable of producing it in the year 3090.

2

1977

There was a knock at the door at the same time the telephone started ringing.

"All right all right, I'm comin'," the woman shouted from the kitchen of her third floor condominium in Boca Raton, Florida. Company? She stopped slicing onions, rinsed her hands, and turned down the volume of the stereo. Fercockta disco music. Who comes to visit at this time of day? She mumbled to herself as she left the counter where she was slicing onions for an egg salad sandwich. The King had died and she was a wreck. The stench wafted their sulphur laden odors through the quaint one bedroom one bath unit, her eyes were moist because she'd been crying. Elvis died yesterday. Who the hell shows up at this time of day. It was two pm, and the summer sun was glaring through her sliding glass door which faced the south west. She yelled out: "Hang on, I gotta get the phone," and took a couple steps to where it sat on the kitchen table. Picking up the handpiece she said, "Hang on someone's at the door," without letting them reply. She would have drawn the blinds, the damn air conditioning bill was ridiculous, but hurried over to the door. Maybe it's a repairman she thought. Damn thing was making funny noises, maybe they-- the condo association--finally got someone to look at these things. Eh, she thought, you never know. "I'm coming," the woman said.

She put her left eye up to the peep hole and stared out. That was the next to last thing that went through her mind. The first was a bullet from a silenced twenty two caliber pistol in the hands of a man dressed as a construction worker. In typical go anywhere universal access attire. Khaki trousers, a baseball cap, clipboard, an orange bucket--where he'd hidden the gun beneath some rags--and beige work-boots. Who'd question a worker bee at a condo? "Just checking on unit fill in the blank," he said to the rent-a-cop security staff who held the door open for him.

The second shot to the door's lock sounded like a phone book hitting the carpeted floor. The hollow point blasted the Schlage apart. The man looked from side to side--nothing. He smirked to himself as if it's just what he'd expected, and as with most South Florida communities that sound wouldn't perk an ear of a nosy neighbor. Condo commandos--the visitor knew--were busy making sure someone wasn't parked in an unassigned spot, or the wrong color person was in the lobby.

He pushed in the door with a gloved hand, shut it behind him, and stepped over the dead woman. He saw her purse on a chair in the kitchen, opened it, inspected its contents, and replaced them. He returned to the corpse, took off her shoes, and removed a pair of inserts, and held them up to the window. They could have been made of plastic, but the visitor knew better, they were amber colored, and and instead of reflecting the light absorbed it. He removed a vial of fluid from his pants pocket, unscrewed its top, and dabbed a few drops of its contents onto a napkin, and rubbed it onto the shoe inserts. Then he held them both up. After a few moments the shoe inserts began to glow, and emit a humming tone. In the midday sun he could see a beam of light of such intensity he had to put on sunglasses. The beam extended from the sky, through the window, on to the woman's carcass, and within seconds, her body was bathed in orange light, and with a barely audible pop--she was vaporized. All that remained was her clothing and a shimmering wall of distorted light the size of a full-length mirror in front of the condo's splintered door. It was transparent and rippled from ceiling to floor and bent the light just so that it reflected the day's western sunlight.

Is it murder to kill someone who wasn't ever really born?

The visitor considered this as he looked around the unit's kitchen. He blithely studied the contents of her refrigerator, took a bottle of cola, sat down at the kitchen table, and picked up the telephone.

He dialed the number he'd committed to memory sixty years earlier and said a carefully rehearsed phrase. He stepped over the dead woman's clothing, and walked slowly into the wall of rippling light. Merging into it as if it was a pool of water whose texture was the fabric of reality. A space between spaces.

The portal disappeared with an inaudible, yet visibly striking snap just as the man's heel passed through it.

3

1958 The Chiropodist

Hello my name is Duss, Herman Duss, chiropodist. I want to tell you about the darndest day I ever had. It was in August of 1958, and a doozy of a scorcher of a day too. I was a young chiropodist then. Much older in many ways then, than I am now. I know, I know, it sounds strange, but let me tell you what happened:

My office--in a small town on the second floor of the medical building--the only one in town--was across the hall from the dentist, and the GP. There was a chiropractor up the hall for a spell, but he got himself run out of town for sleeping with the sheriff's wife. Oh those were the times I tell you. I'll get back to that sheriff. But back to that day in August, two men and a woman barged into my office. They said they were on the run and were sent to me from the GPs office, my friend, Doc Beaufort. I was hospitable and let them in. One of them claimed to be from the future. Like any sane man, I thought they were full of baloney, but because maybe the gal razzle dazzled me, or I wasn't busy, or maybe just wanted to be a swell guy, I humored them. Heck I even broke out the office bottle, and gave the jumpier fella dressed like Elvis a tipple and a smoke. Chesterfield, still smoke em. Best cigarettes made. None of that artificial stuff. Oh, right back to `58. These folks tell me that the Sheriff is after them, and that Doc Beaufort, said that I would hide them out for a spell. Since me and the Doc were good friends I obliged, and asked the young filly to get up in my chiropody chair and I would give those feet a look see.

There was a banging on the door, and then I heard the sheriff holler, and those three kids skedaddled out of the office so quick I didn't have a chance to present my bill, so I chased them.

What I saw nearly knocked my socks off, but you had to see it to believe it, and I did:

One by one they disappeared into this wall of glimmering air--looked like one of those mirages in the distance--you see on a hot day on the highway. I jumped in, and instead of being right behind them I was someplace altogether different. Like Alice jumping through the rabbit hole, but I was in the same place I'd been. However, it had changed, like decorators came in and redone the place in a jiffy. I was in my own office, but it was someplace I'd never known, my Naugahyde chair was gone, there was some other sort of equipment in its place. There were all sorts of shoes and shoe inserts. I picked up a pair, what the heck were these? I held a pair up to the light, darndest thing I'd ever seen.

I felt gosh awful, like I'd eaten some rotten food, or maybe had a few too many tipples. I scratched my head, and went looking for the office bottle when some fella appears out of one of my old exam rooms. He looks at me like I busted in--a colored guy--he comes at me like he's gonna beat me. You never know with these people.

"What're you doing here?" I say.

"What am I doing here," he thumps his chest like some big gorilla--like he owns the place. "What are you doing here? You don't have an appointment."

"What are you talking about sonny," I said. "You're in my office. Either get out or I'll call the law on you."

"This is my office. And you're trespassing." He said.

That big Negro, dressed up like a fancy high falutin sort, suit coat and tie, and I didn't want no trouble. This was no place for coloreds I started to tell him, when he shoved me into the waiting room. It had all been rearranged too. I'd never seen anything like it. All coloreds and women in short skirts. Where the heck was I?

He told me that I must have been lost, and tossed me out of my own place. What nerve. Gosh darn young whipper snapper tossed me out into the hallway. I looked at the sign on the door, and I tell you it was as if a family of spiders with frozen legs crawled on up my spine. It wasn't my name! I didn't know what to do, but I did know my neighbors. The dentist?

Sure he'd be there, I could still smell that dentists office smell, and when I went and looked at the name plate--same as me--he wasn't there anymore. Oh my gosh.

Maybe the GP was there. I went over to Doc Beaufort's office. Imagine my relief when I saw his name still on the door. Thank goodness. I opened the door, and it was exactly the same as it was yesterday when Doc Beaufort and me played a game of checkers. I went up to the pebble glass window, and saw Milly, his wife, girl friend, nurse, I never figured out which, but she was there; pretty as ever, and she looked at me real funny.

"Herman," she said. I could hear the concern in her voice. "I think the Doc is going to want to see you." She stood up, walked around the counter, opened the door, and shooed me into an exam room lickety-split. Oh my goodness this was not going to be good. Maybe I had a stroke or a heart attack. I didn't know what to think. I felt around for a Chesterfield, and took the pack out, put one in my mouth and was just about to light up when Beaufort came into the room. He looked just like he did yesterday. That was a relief.

"Well well well, Herman Duss. Do you know where you've been for the last twenty years?"

"What?" Was Doc Beaufort funnin' me? Was this a trick question? Maybe he had something to do with those scoundrels who made off without paying their tab.

"Herman, there's no easy way to tell you this, so I'll just spell it out. You stepped through a portal into the year 1978."

"But you look the same as you did yesterday. So does Milly, come on lay off the jokes."

"I don't age, either does Milly."

"Nah." He had to be funnin' me. Everything seemed the same in the office as it did yesterday, or did it?

I looked around, and there were some gadgets I never imagined existed. He stood there and stared at me, then opened the door, and called Milly. "Can I go back?"

"Bring me some IM diazepam."

He gave me a shot and I calmed down a bit, but had so many questions I didn't know where to start.

"Herman, that portal you stepped into, the one where the three folks entered was an entry to another dimension. You know what that is, right? You watch the Twilight Zone--we've talked about that many many times."

That much was true. Beaufort and I had spoken about time, space, Sputnik, and he told me that some day there would be such a thing as rockets that go off into space, and that some day people would invent all sorts of things.

This is when he floored me. I guess the shot was some kind of tranquilizer because I swear I would have had a heart attack. He said that he himself, and Milly were really from the year 2070, and that the fellas and gal that I followed were also from different times.

"Are they here?" I asked.

"No, they were altered so they could travel through time and retain their memories, and a few other things."

"What other things?"

"Herman this isn't going to be easy for you. Do you remember the Fairy Tale of Rumpelstiltskin?"

"The fella who fell asleep for a while and slept through all sorts of things . . . are you saying that I--"

He held up a hand mirror and I saw my face. I was older. What happened to me?

It was as if he read my mind: "Yes, you slept in a state of suspension between times and spaces."

"No. That can't be. Where did I go?"

"You traveled through time without being prepared and fell into a coma of sorts, just suspended between moments."

"Why can't I remember anything?"

"You're body isn't equipped for time travel," he said.

"Can you fix it?" I asked.

He didn't answer me, but I knew that I would not see my lost youth again. That was gone.

"Can I go back?"

"No. Herman, you can't. You're to remain here--now in 1978."

"There must be something that hole has still got to be there. That hole should take me back to 1958, right?"

"Oh it's there Herman, but you'll go back to a place that's not going to be the same, you're not the same. The fact that the world went on without you the day you disappeared in 1958 changed the arc of history-- yours, the fellas in the building, the sheriff who banged on your door that day-- "

"You know about that? Where is the sheriff?"

"He's gone Herman. Never to be seen again. 1958 went on without you, and you were replaced."

"What do I do, where do I go?"

"Well well well, the fact that you emerged here, today, means that something has to be done. You aren't dead."

"But I was gone. What happened to my office, my family, my wife?"

"They went on without you, Herman."

"Well what can I do now?"

"I don't know. Why don't you lay back, shut your eyes, and I'll figure out what we can do for you."

4

MILLY AND BEAUFORT in 1978

"We have to do something with him," Milly said.

"I know, I know. Let's let him sleep while I check the alternative histories. What his presence at this time means right now, nothing good can come of his presence here, now."

Milly said: "Where does he belong?"

"Nowhere," Beaufort said. "But we have to put him somewhere, to send him, my my my, this is a most vexing event."

"We can always just send him forward."

"I'd have to add the mymine chips."

"Or some version, his tissue isn't prepared. We'd need to educate him--let him see what's happened since

1958 before setting him out into the world. He's got nothing, nowhere to go."

"I know, he just vanished twenty years ago."

"And that was the end of him, here. He supposedly ran off and never was heard of again--at least that's how history's gotten his life trajectory recorded."

"He's not equipped to know what he doesn't know-- his mind may melt, he could die, or do something that could toss history so off-kilter that we could end up never being born."

"Prepare the cocktail Milly. We've got to alter him before he does anything stupid, and take our chances. The computers will sort it out."

Duss had other plans.

He hated coloreds, always had, always would, and the fact that one had taken his office meant he'd a score to settle.

5

Doc Beaufort's Dilemma

Something had to be done with Duss soon, and the logical choice was to contain him.

He was a 1958 human, with all that came with his aging process, presence of mind, and ambitions. His youth had dissolved into an unhealthy middle age, and despite having gone astray--fallen off the tracks recognizable by the supercomputers in orbit--there was no history of the life and times of Herman Duss.

I was not inclined to be be hasty in choosing to maintain his absence from human life, although allowing him to remain in a suspended state was compelling, it was, unfeasible. He had to be altered, and sent from 1978 to 2070, and be re-educated, reconditioned, and reassigned to a place in history where his presence would not alter what was, or what would be. Therefore, I readied the now unconscious man for modification.

Genetic modification entails the addition of a cyclic nucleotide. There are four in naturally born human beings: adenine, guanine, cytosine and thymine. A combination of three make up the rungs of the DNA ladder. The triplets are translated within the cells to amino acids, then proteins, which nearly all bodily functions rely.

The man made marvel, mymine, a cyclic nucleotide was developed to integrate into the makeup of all cells, and could alter the aging process, eliminate disease, and form neural pathways enhancing sensory function. Mymine nucleotides are driven by orbiting supercomputers which have been self-developing since the early part of the Thirtieth Century.

The degradation endured by ordinary tissue traveling through accelerated time is rapid disintegration. Apoptosis--a cellular death akin to shedding--and resultant demise of the organism.

Duss needed to be altered, to be sorted out by the supercomputers which account for almost all history. The slightest change, say in 1765 can, and often does have ramifications beyond that epoch.

The supercomputers equilibrate the variables, accounting for acceptable modifications, but do not allow for gross disruptions.

Time incursions can result in the demise of a subject. Tampering with events as they might hinder the outcomes resulting in their--the developers, the computers--the existence of a future which is self perpetuating are not permitted.

I had begun the preparations to modify Duss, readying the proper equipment as proscribed. I was not giving him full strength regenerative mymine so as not to allow for cellular reintegration beyond , two, three, maybe four, more leaps through any one of the thousands of portals.Before physical decay sets in.

The mymine used on Duss is temporary, although it can be integrated permanently if deemed appropriate. But this was not my intent, or at my discretion.

He had to be evaluated by my monitors in 2070--a permanent modification is not up to me. Too many variables need to be assessed.

Duss's alteration by design was temporary. There was no place in this era for a man enhanced via the power of the orbiting supercomputers, and unless he could be scanned, programmed, and his linear trajectory through history calculated, who knew? This could have profound ramifications.

I did not have the particular equipment to perform such analysis until 2010. I had to work fast, anything could happen now--he couldn't be set out into the world--no, not with what he might alter.

His implanted nano-chips begin cellular integration immediately, and can last approximately 120 days, the ordinary life span of a red blood cell.

Erythrocytes consist mainly of hemoglobin, a complex metalloprotein containing heme groups whose iron atoms temporarily bind to oxygen molecules (O_2) in the lungs and release them throughout the body. Its quaternary structure incorporates four chains of protein. An ideal cell for transport of the mymine generated, and integrated proteins. The host's circulatory system can be driven by nanochips devised solely for time travel, and can be removed and replaced--if warranted--before being plucked out by the spleen, and destroyed. This will prevent Duss from fully integrating the altered DNA into all his tissues, and allow transport so he can be dealt with in the future.

Mymine, once installed is fully functional throughout the lifetime of a human being, and self generates with the cell cycle of all humans who've been permanently altered. All human beings born after 2040, have, by way of mutations during mitosis, cellular division, a permanently guided metabolism. Prophase, metaphase, anaphase--the separation of the cell spindle, and finally telophase allowing for the production of new cells with fully integrated nucleotides.

We readied our equipment in 1978 in such a manner to allow Duss a rudimentary awakening from his chemically induced coma. Yes I did only give him diazepam at first, but when he awoke Milly and I couldn't project any record as to what or whom he would become. It was imperative to get him to a portal that led to 2070 before he could utilize any of the knowledge stored in parts of his brain the nano-chips would awaken.

He would have heightened conscious awareness, telepathies, a degree of telekinesis, and heightened intellect. The modified red blood cells would automatically be driven to areas of his body which may have some damage, and a cascades of metabolic events would give him a most salubrious--almost superhuman prowess.

Unfortunately the emotional centers would also be heightened. His preconceptions would be amplified, and the data stored in his unconscious would become accessible to him.

It's obvious why a 1958 chiropodist with powers beyond his ability to comprehend them should not be set out into the world in this era.

Approximately one hour after Duss was infused he went into a rage, destroying the examination room barging into the office which used to be his own, and began pummeling the man of African heritage to within an inch of his life, and swiping who knew what from both offices.

An hour after that there were time currents, subtle at first, but gradually they became more significant.

Both Milly and I, settlers from the year 2070 began to experience surges of unexpected sensory awareness.

Because a time paradox takes a few days to fully take hold, Duss had to be found, and dealt with.

There were people living now; which could be 1978, 1958, 1928, 2070, and many, many, other periods, who resettled, or were vacationing. They could be affected. Now, is a relative term, and a time wave could wash across the space-time continuum. We needed to work fast to prevent what we could.

6

DUSS AWAKES

Negroes. Why? What gave them the right--who, and . . . the first thoughts I had when I awoke at the GPs office. I don't know what he gave me, but I dreamt something, he said some bullpucky about being from the future. He and that girlfriend, nurse, whatever, they were both from the future.

Bullpucky? Maybe, maybe not. Something clicked in my way of thinking and I could think in a way I could not recall. I felt smarter. Those were my first thoughts that day back in `78. But that day I remember so clear because it was as if I was an older fella in younger one's body. And my mind, my thoughts. Aww heck, I knew things that I never knew I knew. I mean I could figure out things so fast it was like I'd had twenty cups of coffee. Holy smokes!

I sat up put my feet on the ground and took a few steps. Oh my this was spiffy. I had a spring in my step that was like I was back in high school. I looked in the mirror and nearly made in my pants. I was young again! I was young, I was smart, I didn't know yet what else I could do, but it was like being Superman from the comics. I didn't know if I could fly--maybe? I'd check that later, but now I had to get squared away with that colored fella that took over my office. I had to go get me some clothes first.

Beaufort left me in this treatment room in my skivvies. I peeked out the door and nobody was there, and went on into the hallway. I heard Beaufort and Milly over to the front desk talking at each other, and tiptoed back into the Doc's private consultation room.

I knew there was a back door out into the hallway, and knew he had some clothing in there. He always had clothing because he was one swell dresser. I shut the door behind me, and I tell you now that there were plenty of gizmos in that room. I grabbed a pair of trousers and a shirt from his closet, there were some shoes in there too--they fit just fine, and while I was dressing saw this machine on his desk.

That was one heck of a machine. I didn't know it then, but sure found out soon.

A typewriter hooked up to a box with a TV screen. I don't know how I knew what to do but just started into typing, and the screen lighted up. It was some kind of an information box, and within a few minutes I knew how to work it. I learned all sorts of things. Things that happened in 1958, and on, and before that. More and more and couldn't believe that I was so full of ideas, thoughts, and that history was a thing, not just words written in books. It was something I could move in and out of. I saw the map on Beaufort's wall, it was a map of portals. I don't know HOW I knew what they were, but I knew that they were doors into other times. I ripped a portion of it from the wall, grabbed whatever I could from the drawers, I was never a thief, or anything like one, but I knew that whatever was done to make me younger, more fit, springier in my step, made me know I needed things. Things only Beaufort would have here at his desk.

My gosh what I'd now known made me gush. Everything I read, every image on the screen, I had to know, and read, and comprehend.

Whatever medicines he'd given me did something gosh awful strong. I had to have it, more of it, and rifled through Beaufort's desk, his cabinets. There, were some containers, sealed like there was some sort of poison or atomic material was in it. I took as much as I could find and shoved it in my pockets.

I didn't know then exactly what it was only that it was something very valuable, something that altered me. I heard them speaking my hearing was profound. They were so far away. Gosh, I think I could have heard ant's footsteps.

This frightened me at first. My senses were sharper. I felt the containers I'd taken--the radioactive stuff--

yes, this must be what changed me into what I'd become. This was fantastic. Some super drug!

I knew that I would recall everything I'd seen. It would all be there when I was beating that jigaboo silly, and then, Ha. It was mine, everything.

The world, just like that became smaller, and I was strong, stronger, more powerful. Amazing. I felt like a superhero from a comic book.

I could now set things like never before. I'd find those scamps who came to my office, and fix them just fine. I realized in those few minutes since awakening change the world. I heard footsteps, Beaufort and Milly, and crouched down. I heard the concern in their voices, something about restraining me. No. Not now, not ever.

The door opened and Beaufort stood there holding up his hands, palms facing me. Trying to calm me down, to relax.

I heard him think that this was going to be a challenge

"I hear you think Beaufort, stand back!" I said. I just laughed and laughed and took that box--a computer-- and threw it at him hard. I wanted to hurt him before I left. I wanted him to know what I had become. Ha.

I did not want to go back to 1958 just then. I did not want coloreds ever to be pulling strings, and people from the future coming back to visit, to play with us like we were fools, no, that had to stop.

My work was cut out, and I'd start by putting an end to these future freaks who've come to live amongst us. I had a purpose for the greater good of all humans.

This had to be some commie plot, I'd get a medal if I set things right--did I really want medals--what was right?

I would decide that, and I had my ideas of these things. That is when I began my mission--I was given another chance at life, my life recharged, refueled with high-test, and sure wasn't going to whittle corns when there was history that needed to be fixed. Oh did I have some catching up to do. I could travel through time now. Hello to another chance to be a young man.

I patted my pockets again, and just knew that all of time was just a blink away--any time, any place--all mine to do with what I wished. Ha.

7

One Quick Schvartze

James Cleveland "Jesse" Owens was more than an athlete. He was a symbol to the world repudiating the Nazi's claims of White Supremacy. One man singularly pissed off Adolph Hitler so much that he refused to show up for the award ceremony. Rumor had it that Hitler threw a historic tantrum vowing to seek a new sort of revenge upon the world. In fact reliable sources revealed that the Führer was said to have farted a peanut when Owens won one of many events back in 1936. But history's mysteries remained inconsequential as to how this American track and field athlete who'd specialized in sprints and the long jump had help from an unlikely source--his chiropodist. We'll get back to that. First a little background.

Jesse Owens was the youngest of ten children born in Oakville, Alabama on September 12, 1913. He was nicknamed, J.C., because one of his sister's said "Jesse you got corns!" when she saw the unusually large thickened tissue at the soles of his feet. Jesse was nine years old when the family moved to Cleveland Ohio for better opportunities, and as fate would have it, cross paths with and ultimately be treated by the chiropodist, Herman Duss.

Speculation arose to the origins of the name Jesse, and this is the derivation: He got the name Jess? like this: When his first grade school teacher asked his name he said "J.C.", but because of his strong Southern accent she thought he said "Jesse". The name took, and he was known as Jesse Owens for the rest of his life.

As a child and into his teens Owens took different jobs in his spare time: he delivered groceries, cleaned dog droppings from the sidewalks of Cleveland, and loaded freight cars. Occasionally he made deliveries for nefarious characters of noted underworld figures. Often choosing the "colored kid" who could: "Run faster than any flat foot copper in town," as stated by Lefty Ponzetti AKA the Maniac of Mayfield, and crime boss of Cleveland who served 40 years of a life sentence at Alcatraz. Owens was said to have delivered "on time every time."

Tales have been told by many of Cleveland's less criminally inclined population that young Jesse did indeed run fast. In fact it's been said he could run faster:

"Than the fastest police car made." He also worked in a shoe repair shop because his feet often ached horribly, and had yet to cross paths with the esteemed doctor whose attention would change the course of history.

J.C.'s father and older brother worked at a steel mill, and ultimately saved enough money to get young Jesse a visit with Dr. Duss, who, despite what would later be described as racial discrimination, refused to allow young J.C. to soak his feet in the office's foot bath. There was a sign in his chiropody office that read: "No colored's allowed to use foot bath," as well as separate foot treatment tools soaking in gallon size jars filled with blue fluid, a disinfectant of sorts, labeled "for colored folk only" another with no label at all.

Duss allowed the young fellow accompanied by his parents into his office on the outskirts of the city provided payment was made in advance. He was escorted into the modern chiropody office and seated in the elaborate chiropody chair. A most curious examination seat similar, yet markedly distinct from a dental examination chair, in that the chiropody chair was a richly decorated seat with genuine artificial Naugahyde, brass levers and cranks to raise, lower, adjust the back and position of the patient seated. An aesthetic to dazzle any chiropody patient with ersatz gemstones embedded in its seams, that would glimmer in the light, shining in through the second floor windows

There were also secret compartments in the custom chair, where illegal alcoholic beverages could be stored, often a side perk of modern chiropody was using their chairs as liquor seats. Duss was known among the underworld criminal community as a man known to consort with Negroes, and to have a robust "put up your feet for a treatment, and sip some chiropody gin," office.

Young Mr. Owens was most impressed with the chairs special sliding panel, for a "patient" to rest his feet on to be inspected and treated. Beneath the sliding tray was another tray to catch the corn and callus shavings, as well as nail debris that would fall when the good doctor went to work on paring dead skin.

Duss was rumored to be the fastest foot scraper East of the Mississippi. He came to this level of notoriety not so much by his academic prowess, but through his willingness to cater to the less desirable, as in the young Mr. Owens. Rumors at the time were that Duss was a member of the Cleveland chapter of the German Bundt party, as well as a KKK Imperial Wizard. Treating negroes was hardly fitting for a man of such impeccable credentials. However, as Duss was known to say among his intimates:

"Black, yellow, red, I don't care, money's green, and that's all I care about." Which, he summarily accepted from the Owens family on many occasions for his "expert" treatment.

The treatments were the removal of thick dead skin on young J.C.'s feet that formed beneath the metatarsal (long bones of the foot) heads. This was on the soles of his feet just below the bottoms of the base of the toes.

The young man gleefully enjoyed being corn free for weeks at a time after a "shalooping" provided by Herman Duss.

To shaloop was the artful swipe of a knife-like instrument with a surgical scalpel blade attached at its end.

Shalooping was as described in the autobiography: "I was a Foot Pioneer," a book published by the Dilcrumb Press--which for a fee would publish anything legible--as a sweeping motion on the foot whittling as such dead skin, or "detritus" which is highly dense keratinized tissue. Very similar on a molecular level to horse hoof, which was temporarily stored as there was little use for it until the Great Depression when it was sold by the pound to several nefarious soup kitchens throughout the Depression Era kitchens, boiled, and made into a broth. Thus contradicting the rumor that some gelatin was made from cow, or horses hoofs, it was soup. Besides, the fact that every part of a cow was utilized by the processing plant made them nearly impossible to obtain.

The connection of Owens and Duss remained buried for decades. For the purpose of this discourse Duss's mysterious disappearance was largely noncontributory to the waves of history, and his absence from any literature or reference until now has remained unremarkable. Duss was rumored to have dispensed shoe inserts to Jesse Owens early in his life, in addition to addressing the young athlete's bothersome foot conditions.

Owens attended Ohio State University in Columbus, Ohio. It wasn't long until this quick on his feet kid became known as the "Buckeye Bullet," and could have thanked the shoe inserts if they still fit.

Owens won eight NCAA championships--that's for the record books, four each in 1935 and 1936. Owens enjoyed athletic success, and despite his extraordinary abilities didn't get the Red Carpet Treatment. In fact, just the opposite he was subject to the times. And times weren't great to be black in America. He was treated like any other non-white. Poorly, and as a third class citizen. Traveling with the team, Owens was restricted, often remaining in his quarters alone with his dreams, a pack of smokes, and his running gear. Back then plenty of hotels, restaurants, and public places had "white only" signs, and he had to order carry-out food, or eat at "black-only" restaurants. Legend has it that Owens had crossed paths with some of history's greatest blues musicians along the way.

The "blacks-only" hotels were notorious for the all night jams of some of the greats of jazz, and as one master bluesman recalled young JC could belt out a mean guitar riff. One of history's little known facts is that the great B.B. King was said to have composed "The Thrill is Gone", when Jesse Owens turned down his offer to allow the fastest fingers on the slide guitar to join his band.

Owens didn't receive a scholarship to OSU despite his efforts, so he worked part-time jobs to pay for school. Fortunately some may argue to the contrary, but the facts are indisputable, that young Jesse was able to amass a small fortune using his skills making deliveries of dubious content for a former employer. Owens could outrun any human, and Lefty Ponzetti, the Maniac of Mayfield always had a route for young Jesse to earn "decent bank for a mulanyan." The term mulanyan, an Italian term for eggplant, gained popular use by those of Italian descent to describe people of African Heritage. Owens used much of his savings to maintain proper foot care, and in the hands of Dr. Herman Duss, DSC, he would go on to greatness. Duss's cutting-edge shoe inserts always needing modifications, were the cornerstone of Owen's unique style, and jackboot smashing sprint; thus hammering Hitler and his henchmen into shame altering the course of history.

Owens's greatest achievement came in a span of 45 minutes on May 25, 1935, during the Big Ten meet at Ferry Field in Ann Arbor, Michigan, where he set three world records, and tied a fourth. He equaled the world record for the 100 yard dash (9.4 seconds), and set world records in the long jump (26 ft 8 1/4 in/8.13 m, a world record that would last 25 years), 220-yard (201.2 m) sprint, (20.3 seconds) and 220-yard

(201.2m) low hurdles (22.6 seconds, becoming the first to break 23 seconds). In 2005, University of Central Florida professor of sports history Richard C. Crapeauchose declared these wins on one day as the most impressive athletic achievement since 1850.

However, that did not happen. Herman Duss had rendered Mr. Owens corn laden feet into hideously painful pedal appendages. There was no way he could even participate in the events as previous history reflected. Duss's first stop after Beaufort's office was nestling himself in the past carefully appearing as needed, to make for German supremacy. The ripples of this time paradox had begun.

8

The Berlin Olympics

In 1936, Owens arrived in Berlin to compete for the United States in the Summer Olympics.

Adolf Hitler was using the games to show the world a resurgent Nazi Germany. He and other government officials had high hopes that German athletes would dominate the games with victories. The German athletes achieved a "top of the table" medal haul. Meanwhile, Nazi propaganda promoted concepts of "Aryan racial superiority" and depicted ethnic Africans as inferior.

This was how it was written to have happened:

Owens surprised the world--and terrified the Germans--by winning four gold medals. On August 3, 1936, he won the 100m sprint, defeating Ralph Metcalfe, on August 4, the long jump (later crediting friendly and helpful advice from Kuz Long, the

German competitor he ultimately defeated) on August 5, the 200m sprint. After he was added to the 4 x 100 m relay team following a request by the Germans to replace a Jewish-American sprinter. He won his fourth on August 9 (a performance not equaled until Carl Lewis won gold medals in the same events at the 1984 Summer Olympics).

Duss made sure it didn't go that way.

Just before the competitions, Owens was visited in the Olympic village by Adi Dassler, the founder of the Adidas athletic shoe company. He persuaded Owens to use Gebrüder Dassler Schuhfabrik shoes, the first sponsorship for a male African-American athlete. Would the shoe inserts given to him by Dr. Duss fit into these shoes?

The long-jump victory is documented, although reluctantly--Nazis were no fans of the American's of dark pigmentation, especially the filmmakers, but Hitler insisted, and forever memorializing in cinematographic splendor his triumphs along with many other 1936 events. In the 1938 film Olympia by Leni Riefenstahl a must-see motion picture Leni captures the event.

After the war she claimed to very few believers, that she truly was a friend of: "Schokoladen," people, and had little or no interest in the Nazi political beliefs. It was rumored that she is a distant cousin of the late Jimi Hendrix. In fact, the cut Voodoo Child, is said to be a reference to Jesse Owens, and that Crosstown

Traffic specifically referred to young Jesse's work with the Maniac of Mayfield. Furthermore, the very orthotics, or shoe inserts that Jesse Owens was given to wear for the 1936 Olympics disappeared shortly after the race.

Subtle changes and Ralph Metcalfe won the 100m sprint by a fraction of a second.

Duss knew that Hitler's medical team, scientists, and others among his inner circle would need to know about Owens NEAR WIN, and the mysterious shoe inserts.

Duss could shift the energy field emitted from the inserts, and all that happened once happened again, only via the power of Herman Duss's will.

Herman Duss happily stepped into a portal he arranged, knowing he'd altered history, and with a veritable degree of certainty knew that Hitler would know just what to do with the miscible amber colored fluid in the vial next to the shoe inserts he'd placed in Owen's locker.

They would make better use of these things, and he made darn sure they were just where they'd be found, ready to catapult the course of World War II.

9

Popping in and out of History
How the Mystery Substance Evolved

Nicola Tesla, the scientist, to some a true visionary, to others somewhat off-kilter, yet productive worked often with crystals. Other historical luminaries who dealt with what some called "quartzite quackery," were Leonardo Da Vinci, and among the items of the occult, obscure, and divine, Napoleon, Nostradamus, Thomas Edison, Albert Einstein, and Adolph Hitler.

Crystals--it's been rumored--were used to access and open energy fields under the proper conditions, and alter the physical universe. These fields create what is known now as quantum harmonics.

In 1943 Erwin Schrödinger, Nobel Laureate and founder of the quantum theory proposed that all living matter at the cellular level can be thought of in terms of quantum mechanics--pure physics and chemistry. Scientists and biologists struggled to understand and embrace the possibilities of quantum biology. Medical understanding of quantum mechanics: the actions and specific treatments, lagged for decades. Mostly because the role of quantum physics in biology was neither well understood, taught in medical colleges, or poorly understood sounds good, but the truth is--this was complete bullshit. But was it?

Life is a molecular process which operates according to quantum theory. It would follow that the quantum processes of humans with over fifty trillion cells, which interact with all the other energy fields in their environment could be cataloged, observed, and the calculations of each atom of each cell quantified, measured, and predicted as they are exposed to a variety of harmonic variations. Human cells have a quantified energy transfer of a certain number of subatomic elementary particles of matter called fermions, or PHOTONS.

These are discrete packets of energy. Cells and intracellular elements are capable of vibrating in a dynamic manner with complex harmonics. The frequency of which could not be measured and analyzed in a quantitative manner until the 2030's. It is important to understand the mechanism by which this vibrational information is transferred directly from the cell and throughout the organism, and make all of the atoms become singular in their vibrational state. To freeze them--if you will--in a solid transferrable state. This is an identification of the vibrating biologic matter, and the subsequent vibrational transference. This is called the tensegrity matrix of all things living.

All living things have a harmonic, not always in tune with all parts, and the harmonic oscillator operates as a signal transducing system from the individual cell's to the cell's nucleus ultimately the DNA is for as long as the organism lives. Vibrating until acted upon by metronomic generators, that like a conductor's baton, sets them all on the the same tone, the same key, tunes up the orchestra of the organisms cells to play along at the same time. The biological oscillations of the cell from the DNA, this tensegrity of tissue matrix systems allows for the specific transfer of information through the cell, and throughout the organism we have this harmonic wave motion.

The harmonic waves of motion of every cell, it's minute parts in every human, and the atom motions all fall into line on the same chord--they're tuned up if you will--this tensegrity of the human matrix is solidified, and with this, solidification there is a suspension of movement, and therefore biological processes can appropriately be treated without the body's natural mechanisms interfering. New parts installed into the basic makeup of the human body are shifted, new mechanisms to be set in action once the orchestration ceases. The human is truly frozen in place, albeit briefly to undergo a complete shift. The shift I am referring to is the movement though a portal. You see, the portal is a time vortex, very much a black hole which sucks in every atom at the speed of light. For a moment, no more, the human can sustain this, but after a few seconds, the cells deteriorate.

In the 1990s researchers began to explore biology through the prism crystals via quantum harmonic theory. Unfortunately the supercomputing technology didn't exist until decades later.

In the 2020's, the relationship between this phenomenon, and another: portals, previously considered cosmic anomalies became evident. For years the cataloging and registry of portals, or gaps leading nowhere, or so it was believed, became the nexus from which time travel became viable. The portals were once considered geological aberrations, sinkholes, yet outlier theorists pieced together a recurring relationship between the bioelectric field, appearance of portals, and isolated, remote, and less studied occurrences became more frequent. People began disappearing into, and reappearing "altered." Compelling global cooperation in a move toward intense studies. Once dismissed as the fodder for occultists and conspiracy theorists, items akin to the the Bermuda Triangle or some other myth became viable examples of portals--holes in the fabric of reality--around the world, which with the accompaniment of the crystalline material could be duly cataloged, mapped, and studied. A portal could be opened or shut, and it's destination duly registered.

At first this phenomenon was easy to dismiss, but as the world's resources diminished, and wars raged on, the ability to travel through time, relocate and with the aide of supercomputing, made for a shift in human history unlike any paradigm before it.

Because every moment has a unique vibe, harmonic, tone as the earth, solar system, and galaxy moves through the universe, this must be accounted for when shifting from one moment to the next. Ordinarily this is adjusted from second to second. A leap through time greater than that of the organisms lifetime changes that harmonic dramatically, and cell function is disrupted proportionally to accommodate for these variations. Time travelers must be prepared via the exponential calculations and cell modification prior to entering a portal. A person traveling through time needs to be tuned up, or have their body harmonize with the period they'll be visiting. If not, the subatomic structures fail. To ensure cell matrices and processes remain intact, an additional nucleotide was developed to maintain the harmonic of the time they left and adjusts it to the time they arrive at. It's almost like their cells are singing the same song they did ten, twenty a hundred, a thousand years hence in perpetuity. You're either going to be in tune with the times or die. Popping in and out of history could be a snap, right?

10

1936 Berlin

The big deal about Hitler shaking hands only with the German victors and then leaving--quickly--has been the fodder historian's have toyed with for decades. I say: What if he just had to use the crapper? Nonetheless, the historians who mattered--the ones whose accounts were published to ft the Zeitgeist put a racial spin on it. He left stadium, shunning the Negro. Olympic committee officials insisted Hitler greet every medalist or none at all. Hitler opted for the latter and skipped all further medal presentations. Regarding reports that Hitler deliberately avoided acknowledging schvartze victories, likely scenario, that he refused to shake his hand, a zealous reporter quoted Owens as follows:

"Hitler had a certain time to come to the stadium and a certain time to leave."

Maybe, he didn't want to remain a guest of Germany for the duration. He goes on:

"It happened he had to leave before the victory ceremony after the 100 meters, but before he left I was on my way to a broadcast and passed near his box. He waved at me and I waved back. I think it was bad taste to criticize the 'man of the hour' in another country."

The real skinny is that once away from the public eye, Hitler told his cronies how disgusted he was that Owens NEARLY managed to win all those medals. In fact, Albert Speer, Hitler's Frank Lloyd Wright . . . sort of, went on to describe Hitler's hasty exit in a more politically soothing manner. Speer, wasn't big on organic design, Negroes, Jews, or much more than his own gig in Nazi land. Even though the Führer didn't have anything Robie House-like in his Alpine getaway, Speer had a job. Covering for Hitler, was like designing the structures of the Reich. Unlike Wright, Speer went on to grander things. After all Hitler had some deep pockets. "Cheesy design's of a Roman Empire copied style," the architectural critic, Jennifer Aldroni, described Speer's work as second, perhaps third rate, and his designs for the master race cities of the future a throwback to times best forgotten. So much for that. Speer became consequent to his architectural skill, or lack thereof, chief of war armaments, and a minister of sorts. In his own words, Speer later recollected in his memoirs:

"Each of the German victories, and there were a surprising number of these made him happy, but Hitler was highly annoyed by the series of triumphs by the marvelous colored American runner, Jesse Owens. People whose antecedents came from the jungle were primitive, and there must be something devised by the Americans to humiliate us."

Hitler reviewed this, and said in note to Speer: "Their physiques were stronger than those of civilized whites and hence, should be excluded from future games. But Herr Speer, is it possible that the schvartze had some additional assistance by way of a chemical, or a mechanical device?"

Speer responded with a brief note that whatever it was could not be discovered via ordinary means. He suggested taking Owens prisoner. But no, that would not work. After all kidnapping and examining Owens, perhaps dissecting him would reveal some secrets, yet it would cause an international condemnation, and tip the Führer's hat prematurely.

What magic did the Negro possess?

As much as history is written by the victors so much for Nazi historians. For Speer, history hadn't been so kind, as for Hitler, volumes have been written. Neither one of them would find a seat at anyone's Seder table, or a cabinet seat in an Obama White House. Nonetheless, back to the facts, which as WInston Churchill stated: The truth is incontrovertible, malice may attack it, ignorance may deride it, but in the end, there it is. The truth being that Mr. Owens was a remarkable athlete, and Speer, a hack architect.

Owens was allowed to travel with and stay in the same hotels as white people in Germany even though it was Nazi time--where everybody hated everyone not German--Jews and Gypsies especially. Things were cool for Owens. The suggestion by one of Hitler's inner circle was to simply take the Negro and hold him as a spy. Which, was initially Hitler's plan. His team was assembled, doctors, scientists, and a facility secured to secret the Negro off to but, it couldn't be done without bringing undue attention to Hitler, and cast a dim light upon the wonders of the Reich. Something had been done to enhance this black man, and it's discovery would be richly rewarded.

Thus HItler afforded Owens the freedom to travel the Fatherland as he wished, escorted by the finest of Germany's scientists, in particular one woman scientist. She functioned initially in the guise as an Aryan whore. Frau Doktor Dagmar Wissenshaft was one of Germany's premier physiologists, and held doctorates in Medicine, Physiology and Anthropology, and just so happened to be a remarkably striking gorgeous woman. She was to be Mr. Owen's personal escort. Studying anything and everything about this schvartze, and take samples of his body fluids. Ha. The Reich commission on advanced Negro studies program (ANSPA) began in 1936, and did not despite nine years of painstaking research, find much.

However something odd was discovered among the contents of Mr. Owen's locker: Shoe Inserts.

Owens returned to the US, and in a New York City ticker-tape parade on Fifth Avenue in his honor, Owens had to ride the freight elevator at the Waldorf-Astoria to reach the reception honoring him. Owens said, "Hitler didn't snub me, it was FDR who snubbed me. The president didn't even send me a telegram." On the other hand, Hitler sent Owens a commemorative inscribed cabinet photograph of himself. Jesse Owens was never invited to the White House nor were honors bestowed upon him by President Franklin D. Roosevelt (FDR) or his successor Harry S. Truman during their terms. In 1955, President Dwight D. Eisenhower (himself an athlete of note) honored Owens by naming him an "Ambassador of Sports."

11

Back in Germany

The dormitory used by Owens during the Olympics, equipped with a sauna bath, which Owens was known to use both before and after the events, has been restored completely, and in every detail but for one thing. The shoe inserts that were given to him by the chiropodist.

Historical records reflect that Hitler did not shake hands with Owens because of his race. That's incorrect. Hitler may not have been a fan of black folks, but he sure as hell wanted to know how he managed to run so fast. Hitler's quest for the high speed "trick" Mr. Owens used lingered.

The Führer ordered a complete, albeit secretive study of Owen's equipment, personal history--spies were given orders in the US to track down anything and everything about this magic Negro. In Germany, unbeknownst to the athlete busy with one interview, photo shoot, or celebrity tour--arranged no less by the Nazi Party itself under the direct command of the Führer--had to keep the colored man busy while he had him investigated. There could be no "incident" or suspicion of Hitler's intent. In a hastily staged fire alert Owen's quarters had to briefly be evacuated as well as the American's locker rooms. Just enough time for Nazi snoops to plant bugs, and search every square inch of the place. There was something the American's had produced that made this Negro perform as he did, and the Führer wanted it. What science, or magic, or whatever it was that made this man so fast?

Gestapo interviews of anyone and everyone who'd contacted the Negro were surreptitiously conducted. Spies dug deep into the black man's life. During the faux fire at the Olympic Village a discovery was made in Owen's locker.

Something was found that no one had ever seen in all of Germany. They seemed to be made for shoes, and were made of some odd--at least to the Nazis--material. They were shaped like the sole of a foot, but didn't reach the toes. They were not flexible, but could fit in a shoe, and they were coated with some gritty liquid. There was a vial of some amber fluid next to them. They MUST according to Nazi scientists be shoe inserts made with material that MUST be some secret American innovation.

For years the shoe inserts removed from Jesse Owen's locker along with the vial of amber fluid remained a mystery to German scientists. What possible power did they possess? Frau Doktor Dagmar Wissenshaft was assigned by the Führer himself to conduct any and all research to discern what secrets these devices held.

After all, a Negro MUST have used them to perform as he did, to augment his own natural abilities. Yes, this was some grand material, that could in times of war make an ordinary man, extraordinary. Hitler knew this was coming, and this was something he had to fully put to use in his growing military.

He summoned the best of the best scientists, and in private correspondence to his architect and confidante, Albert Speer, he wrote:

"We must find what these things do, and how they do it, and put it to work for us. Surely they are an American secret weapon."

To which Speer replied:

"The schvartze, Owens, was merely a puppet used by the Americans to humiliate us."

What were the inserts made from? What properties did the substance in the vials have?

The day they were confiscated altered the course of history again.

Upon receiving word of the discovery Hitler made public his beneficence, and made it a point to show the world his good sportsmanship. Himmler the racial purist was furious, but as Speer later wrote: "Himmler is an ass mouth fool with no concept of the grand scheme of things. He can go fuck chickens."

12

The First Time Ripple: Hitler DOES Meet Owens and Their Photo Op Makes Newsreel History

By shaking hands with the schvartze the press would be too busy to record the "incident" in the men's dormitory.

The SS had no concerns as the locker room was set ablaze by the soldiers, and although there was minimal damage, nothing was missing, except of course the orange plastic shoe inserts that Jesse Owens must have worn to win so many medals. Ha.

As far as classified Nazi documents go, only a few folks laid eyes on them. The authors and a few others, who often met a premature demise had little to report. Even Frau Doktor Wissenshaft couldn't glean much from the shoe inserts. The experiments with athletes revealed nothing.

What were these things?

She had her subjects one after the other put them in their shoes. Force them to run, jump, and some even attempt--with little if any success--fly.

Many "subjects" were noted to have perished in their feeble attempts of flight. She made note that after tossing several subjects off the roof of the laboratory facility the "failure to achieve" altitude was evident. The thought of faster running higher jumping soldiers remained in a corner of the Führer's mind, but circumstances overcame any preoccupation, that was Frau Doktor Wissenshaft's job.

She remained perplexed for nearly six years, and thousands of subjects. The inserts were deemed worthless by the Doktor, but as many things during that era, she maintained that there might be something to the devices. And in efforts to keep her work funded continued researching the mystery shoe inserts.

In all of her studies the Doktor neglected any examination of the amber fluid in the accompanying vials. The liquid was merely dismissed as a foot lubricant, and nearly discarded. A few drops remained before the laboratory assistant pouring out the fluid was shot for destroying items without authorization.

Reports of spy organizations could find no trace of the insert's origins, and the chiropodist, Herman Duss, was as per the reports of Hitler's spies, no more than an imbecile with no value whatsoever as an asset.

The Führer continued to seek out articles of the occult, obscure, and mysterious as the war turned against the Reich's plans. If not for an accident in Frau Doktor Wissenshaft's laboratory the project would have been scrapped in favor of developing some other weapon, and remained some remnant in Hitler's mind.

In light of the fact that the inserts did absolutely nothing to enhance athletic prowess, there was one curious finding that occurred. When for no reason other than sheer frustration, perhaps boredom, the Doktor alone in her laboratory dabbed some of vial's remaining contents on the shoe inserts. She held them up to the light bewildered at what she found. The findings written in her journal were as follows:

"When the plates are coated with the fluid from the American Negroes vial and are held up to the light of day they begin to hum, and become warm. They generate heat, and act as a prism. A ray of the sun's light is captured by the inserts, and it casts a beam of glowing light in the lab. I find it difficult to breathe."

She stopped writing in her journal and began toying with the inserts. She set them in clamps and began moving them around the lab table. This was something odd. More than she expected.

Suddenly, the orange beam formed a patch of light on the wall. It appeared that the shoe inserts arranged in such a way, one beside the other, like a magnifying glass they captured the sun's light, and formed a beam of some kind. A light amplifier.

The orange lighted surface flared brightly and a gush of some force threw Frau Doktor to the ground.

She watched as the wall bathed in light began to change hues, from very bright to nearly a flame, then it died down to a dull sunset tone. It seemed to radiate some force. Then it became simply an open hole of shimmering light. She stared into it. The room stood still, and the gap in reality began to ripple and contort.

There was a rumbling sound like distant thunder. She looked over her shoulder, the sky was clear--she'd swear to it, and crab walked away from the chasm.

Suddenly the room went silent, and the space widened, and began to draw her toward it. Was she being sucked in? No. Not me, she reached for her life. Maybe find one of the laboratory people from the camps. Send one in. She clawed away from the energy field that was pulling flasks, and papers into it. She felt the tug, and grasped the lab bench, climbed up to her feet.

The inserts were still in place on the bench where she had them clamped in wooden vices just so--she realized what she'd done--opened some door, but to where?

Because Frau Doktor Wissenshaft was of the rank she was, and had a staff whom she could do as she wished with when she wanted, she did.

She hollered out to the guards. "Bring me some subjects!"

A guard poked his head into the lab and saw the orange hole, and ducked out.

"Stop." She insisted that the soldier bring her some of her "assistants" some of the undesirables, a half dozen work camp subjects. "March them into the laboratory."

Within seconds, prisoner after prisoner was shoved into the lab. The guard wanted no part of it. and then one by one, into the stunning orange shimmering light. All of them disappeared briefly, and then reappeared seconds later. She was baffled.

What use could there be for this? They disappear and show up, that's it? How could this make someone run faster, jump higher, do anything except hide for a few seconds. Maybe the military could use this? She used metal objects on her subjects, but this disabled the device. No, not good for soldiers. Too slow for the "other" relocation process the Reich had engaged.

Because of what some historians from the future reflect as German stubbornness, the connection between the fluid in the vials and the inserts remained separate.

The ripple in time was subtle, yet the effects significant nonetheless. The butterfly's wings had flapped. Duss succeeded in shaving a moment from one man's time, and tweaking the lives of others nearly a century later.

13

The man from another time: CP

It was late, the sun had set, the company left, and we made our way to the bedroom. We screwed for an hour, hit at least ten positions, a few I'd never think existed, but they did, and lay there afterwards smelling of funky steamy crotch. I ran my hand through her hair, onto her shoulder, and along the smooth curve of her flank onto her thigh. She kissed me quick on the cheek, got up to go to to the bathroom, and I fell asleep.

I awoke in a king sized bed in a room bathed in a yellow tinged light shining in through an open window. The curtains gushed in on a warm breeze that felt thick and humid. I heard the the sea rushing ashore and retreating. Birds chirped, flapped their wings, paused to ride a thermal and dive. I sat up and breathed in the ocean's fresh air.

I looked around bedroom. It could have been a suite at a high end hotel, but it wasn't. The impersonal utilitarian amenities weren't there, no minibar, or fire escape map on the door--personalized too, a seashell rimmed photo--I squinted and made out a family--not mine, whose? This was a private home with knick knacks, photos, a desk, and an oceanfront view. Couldn't have been mine. After all I lived under a bridge just outside the city. Must have been the booze, but the outlines of memory began to form. I looked at the space beside me, someone was there. Was she in the bathroom? I held my breath a few beats, nothing. I studied the indentation next to me on the bed, felt it, sniffed it--still warm, and smelled of musk, and some floral bouquet.

Why couldn't I remember? I rubbed my chin. Blackouts weren't alien to me, but something about this place was off-kilter, almost otherworldly. Was I me? I got dressed quickly, and although the clothing fit, I couldn't recall them being my own. I made my way out, grabbing a pen from the desk and a few sheets of paper--If this was a dream I wouldn't be able to write, if not I had to take notes--I opened the door slowly and stepped into the hallway.

The air was a few degrees cooler, and smelled like new car. I looked left, right, and left again. Long hallway, a stone floor and narrow series of rugs that looked like a few hundred Iranian kids went blind making them, were between me and the staircase. There were paintings on the walls every few feet. Some I recognized as museum pieces, others were a style I'd never seen, but I'm no expert. I didn't know how I knew what I knew then, and didn't care. I just wanted to know what the fuck was going on. Who's place was this?

"Hello," I could hear my own voice bounce off the walls, "Is anyone here?" My voice echoed.

There was a crystal chandelier above an immense sprawling staircase. I took it one step at a time, stopping on each to listen. Was I alone? "Hello, is anyone here?" Nothing, just the sound of my feet on the marble stairs. I stopped in the foyer, and looked around, there was a hallway leading to the double front doors. I tried opening them--they were locked--there was a keypad, but I didn't know the sequence to punch in. What the fuck?

I banged on them in a futile frenzy. The sound resonated like I was locked in. A minute or so I don't know how long, but finally I stopped, righted myself, and figured there was some explanation to this. All of it. What the fuck? I stopped to collect myself--whoever the fuck I was--my memory was off.

A Rothko hung on the wall, a Monet next to it, and a Van Gogh, in an alcove, a small table with a lamp glowed to display the painting. I spun around, calculated how much they'd be worth as I stared at the rippling marble staircase and felt dizzy. Something crept over me--I had to move--I didn't belong here. My legs were wobbly, but I kept going. A grand open living space with high ceilings, more rugs, ornate sculptures--more collector's pieces, but whose? I didn't care then, but knew I'd care later, if only I could get the fuck out of here, get my shit together. Focus. I had to know where dreams end and reality begins. I needed confirmation that I'd awoken, or been taken-- to what, where, why? I kept moving, something from deep inside told me to get the fuck out of here. I'd felt imminent danger before, and was feeling it now.

Another room, a ballroom, a grand piano, more artwork, sculptures out of some material I couldn't imagine existed. I looked up to see a huge amber colored stained glass window. I didn't know what the images on it were, or consider them at all. I could smell something else, a cloyingly sweet smell, it had to be the kitchen. There had to be another way out of here. Although uninhabited, the immense Manse must have had--I would've checked the whole place out--amenities I could use, but not now. I pushed open a pair of doors from where the smell came from.

Odd minimalist decor looked inviting, comfortable, yet not like anything I could recall. The walls that weren't adorned with fine art were windows without blinds, overlooking the sea. I poked around, shouting out if anyone was around. I patted my pockets to see if there was anything on me to spike a memory-- anything--did I have something to remind me of who I was, where I came from--shit, I hadn't a clue. I had to get out of there, but something lingered, as if I was drawn to the place. There a flat screen TV of sorts--a glowing pane the size of a door, a series of numbers and a talking head. I looked away to the rest of the kitchen. Plumbing fixtures at the sink looked like something that could purify dirt and turn it to drinking water. The stove--a Viking, or some generation of the brand? The refrigerators, a wall of them would have looked equally sterile and futuristic if they didn't have that personal human touch. Photos. Silly pictures drawn in crayon stuck on with magnets. I looked closer. I could see the reflection of my face in the metal door, and a face in one of the pictures.

Shit . . . it was me! I was in this picture in this fucking house, and there was a woman, a beautiful woman. Motherfucker. What happened to me? I saw a note on the table, it was written in the personal scrawl reserved for teenage women, spouses, or lovers, and on it I saw my name, and a series of numbers, and a word. Shit. I held up the letter to the to the light, and studied it.

Some fragments of a reality started to form, and the empty place in the bed were just starting to make sense. Yeah, it was a hangover, right? Yes, and then it felt like the earth began trembling. An earthquake? Nothing had fallen from any shelves, there was no movement of the room, or the floor I stood on.

Something happened that shook my mind the way barometric pressure shifts before a hurricane. Either my optic nerve was being desiccated by a death beam, or some slow acting poison was kicking in. The numbers she'd written began to fade, the room started spinning, I grabbed the photo off the ice box and jammed the note in my pocket and I ran. I ran as if a sniper was firing at me--I had the numbers in my head. My eyes and my mind weren't rotting, no, it was the fabric of reality.

There was a flash. Something that caught my eye on the way out the doors--a blast of light hit the corner of my visual field--I turned to look at the TV screen. I paused just briefly, and before the next blast of reality kicked in I saw it, and it was something that set off a cascade ideation, I stared at the pane--a fraction of a second was all it took--in one crystallization, the day's news, time, and date.

14

2070

I punched in the numbers on the keypad, there was a beep, beep, beep, and they sprung opened. I stepped out, squinted at the bright yellowish sky, gradually my eyes adjusted to the light, and I looked around. The grounds as grand as the home. I looked around, and rubbed my chin. That was still there. Nothing else I had on me reminded me of who I was, or where I'd come from. I could at least feel my face.

Vicissitude occurs on my face when I haven't shaved, I get cramps in my gut when I drink cheap booze, and my feet hurt when my shoes don't fit. Seasons change, puppies grow into dogs, kittens to cats, and questions unanswered leave a gap in my mind the way vermin gnaw at your toes when you're tied up in some perverts dungeon. But my feet weren't around any vermin and my soles ached so bad I had to sit down. It felt like there were stones in my shoes so I took them off along with my argyle socks and sat down on the stone ledge surrounding a fountain. Water sprayed in the breeze from the bronze bare chested woman's breasts. Some sculpture. Then again everything about this was off. Maybe it was the color of the sky-yellow. Or the way people: groundskeepers, servants, who knew, were dressed, in white sparkly jumpsuits. Or the fact that it the year 2070 and I hadn't a clue as to how I'd gotten there. There were things I did know I don't know how, but I did.

I didn't always have bum feet, but I'd been walking around semi-dazed for the last two hours exploring this wacky world that I wasn't born into. I was a child when the the Space Shuttle Discovery was still orbiting, computers had become a part of life, and internet porn put sleazy dirty movie houses out of business, and everyone yacked and texted on cell phones.

I'd awoken to a place in history that hadn't happened yet, at least not in my life. Maybe it did and I didn't recognize it because it occupied another dimension that existed simultaneously with my own. I didn't have a clue it was all confusing, and I was lost, disoriented, and my damn feet hurt. They didn't hurt when I rolled out of bed and the gal next to me couldn't wait for me to return from the can,no. I recall the bed, and more kinky sex. The sheets were made of some funky material out of a Star Wars episode and tossed aside. It seemed like it lasted for hours but was really less than a minute, and then she went back to sleep. I grabbed my clothes and headed out to catch the lay of the land. The house was quiet and dark, but may have looked like something from the Jetsons. Reality as I know it, was just off. I stepped outside and the brisk breeze of static electricity made my hair stand on end. I needed coffee, and maybe a shot of hooch. Where the fuck was I, and how did I get here. And who the hell was that broad in the sack?

No one was around so I helped myself to one of the puzzling looking vehicles. There were cars but they weren't like anything I'd seen in my lifetime, and they sure didn't work the same way either. I could see the outline of a city, and decided to hoof it into town. Maybe there'd be some answers there, maybe not. But after that funky sex and lack of coffee I wasn't sure this was where I belonged. Oh, what made the sex so funky? The broad and I didn't even touch at first she sort of hovered over me, and took on some translucent glow, and the next thing I knew we were intertwined like pretzels, then it was over, like I said it lasted less than a minute. I timed it with the second hand of my watch, the only thing that made any sense.

I'd had it for over a decade a trusty timepiece. One that stays on your wrist for a reason rather than seasons or style, it works, and my ancient Rolex told me it was time for a drink. So I thought about where I was, how I got there, the nearest bar and a phone might help. I had calls to make, thoughts to sort through. I've been hungover plenty in my days, I've blacked out, but I always has a hangover. Not today, this was something else, and I couldn't stop thinking about the broad who wasn't there. Usually, after a night with a broad she's around in the AM, and there's no sex like morning sex. Damn, I couldn't stop thinking about her just like that, no sinewy shadow and warm flesh, not a feel to cop. A phantom screw with a roboslut I'd met the night before. No, I knew that much it was more, just how much more? I had to figure this out. I didn't have amnesia, I just couldn't remember what happened yesterday.

I walked along and thought, but there were gaps in my mind's eye. It was as if pieces of memory had been whittled away, that the past didn't shape up the way I thought I recalled it. Back to the woman:

Even if it didn't seem like I touched her I saw her in my mind's eye her nipples dancing around in a silk sack, her hair falling across her face, her lips, her eyes, her waist, and that snatch. So perfect its smell lingered the musky sweet fecund smell, the lingering taste of a floral nest of flowers and beast. Sweet, sour luscious viscous fluids filled my mouth, and the heady flesh's flavor embedded in my mind making my ears burn and heart race. I still smelled her on my upper lip and tasted her, and felt a wave of blood fill my cock and my thoughts made no sense just a madness that'd taken over every sense. Just one more smell of her neck, her chin, her thighs . . . But no. She was gone. I leaned back in the seat of some vehicle that hadn't been invented yet, and shut my eyes.

15

GRINDER

"What the fuck?" His eyes opened like someone jabbed a hot poker to his flank. He woke up to the sound of his own snoring, and he sure wasn't going to let on it wasn't him. This is a man who's always ON even when he's alone.

How ya doin'? The name's Grinder, Neal Grinder, you can pronounce it the way James Bond does in that cool creeping background music way if you want to get the full impact of what I'm all about, dig? Whatever.

So I got out of the sack today, took a leak, combed my hair, first things first, shaved, carefully trimming my Elvis sideburns, and took a slug of booze-not much, just enough to face the day-and realized I had no freaking idea where the fuck I was. That ain't an unusual thing for me because I'm an on-the-move kind of guy. Yesterday's gone, today's here.

Something funky happened. Maybe a dream, maybe the dope and booze--I didn't give a rat's ass, but I did check to see if my wallet with my ID, loot, and C-phone was still there. Check A-Okay, and a message to boot.

I was feeling weird, and even though the place smelled good, like a broad. But there was no one in the sack--she must've left--I don't even remember if I was with a slut last night. Eh, no big deal. I was wondering if my car was okay, that's the first shit I was gonna give this morning. I looked around the room, it was an old hotel, and outside the window it was on the ocean--fuckin' A, beachfront digs. Not bad. A real dump though, I can see from the window the joint was slated for demolition. There were signs along the beach. Something told me--don't ask what it was--maybe that voice in my head saying I was in the wrong place, and had to bust a move outta here. I pulled on my boots, and unlike the terlet at the motel I checked into a few days ago, this joint had antique plumbing. What the fuck? I was in a run down, fancy, high falutin Ritz Carlton type joint, where the furniture looked like it could've cost as much as my ride when it was new. Old junk, but so was my ride, that'd be a classic 1959 Cadillac rag top. That's right baby, Candy Apple Red. Cream leather and fins the size of a donkey's dong.

How did I end up at this joint? Hey, I didn't give a shit, because yesterday me and my buddy had some outrageous shit happen. We're both doctors, and both unemployed, unemployable, and these days being

MDs isn't what it was ten, twenty, years ago. I was on the dole--collecting disability benefits for psychiatric reasons--yeah, right. As if any sane man or chick would want to see patients in these times. Then again I wasn't alone. Plenty of guys doing the same boogie. My pal CP's on the same plane, only he ain't cashing in, so we do a little doctoring on the down low here and there. They call it locum tenens in the legit world, We call it fill in for someone who pays us cash for seeing patients.

Yesterday I remember we had some gig seeing old geezers at a nursing home, and got lost, ended up in some podunk hick town outside the city. I don't know if what happened yesterday was real--and that's one big friggin' if--I done traveled through time. The way this joint looked I was in the 1920s. But since my cell phone was working I knew I was smack dab in the time zone I'm supposed to be. Shit, that was maybe some funky dope, and I tagged along on some funky trip.

I'm ready to split and the door, it's locked. And see these paintings on the walls. Shit. They gotta be museum pieces on face value alone I could make some serious bank hocking these bad boys with my fence Lenny. But seeing as how I wasn't sure where I was, I made a mental note they were there. I could always come back for them.

I was just putting my brain cells to work as to who the artists were, when it dawned upon me that something beyond real funky happened yesterday. It wasn't my ordinary funkiness. Ordinary for me is a good day at the track, some poker, and following up with a night at the tit bars. Maybe taking a ho to share my bed with. I looked over at the bed . . . What the fuck?

I knew there was no ho, just real expensive lookin' shit right outta some Bed Bath and Bullshit. Pricey looking rags. I looked out the window on the other side of the room. Marone!

I took another pull from the pint bottle of sour mash. Marone! There's this long stretch of neatly trimmed bushes and hedges on a manicured lawn that went on forever, and a fountain and pool smack dab in the middle of the yard that looked like something from Architectural Indigestion. Where the fuck was I?

Bits and pieces were coming to me, but seeing as how I tend to blank out most nights I was dealin' with some slim pickin's in the brain department. I do remember a card game, and smelled of smoke that was in the room. Something happened and it was big, and the harder I tried thinking more and more shit came into my head as if I'd taken some drug. Something was going on with my mind that was different, and I knew I was on the edge of some level of thinking I ain't been at. It felt like I was on a wall, climbing up, and catching a glimpse over it. Just a flash of something or another of a whole new world or planet or something. It was like I was getting off on acid or some other high powered dope, but didn't have the full dose to get me over the wall. Close but I wasn't getting off. Maybe some coffee, or a line of coke or something.

I figured an investigation into things was in order and went looking for my jacket. Leather baby, smooth Calfskin. Since I slept in my clothes I didn't have to worry about getting dressed. My shoes were off, and I didn't know where those motherfuckers were, and went into looking when I heard a knock on the door. I froze. Who the fuck is that?

16

GRINDER SKIPS OUT

I stood still. Didn't budge--nada, not even a blink-- and waited. Who the fuck could that be? My pal CP? Nah, that fucker wouldn't knock, he'd just open the frigin' door and come in.

I didn't know where I was or what I was doing there, and whoever was at the door was probably not there to turn down the sheets and say dinner is served. I don't think I picked up a dame last night, went to her pad and banged her. THAT I would've remembered, so I split.

I remember being with my pal CP yesterday, he was with some dame gettin' all hot and heavy. Maybe they clicked and skedaddled, maybe not. Any who, I had to boogie. I didn't need any heat. After all I was on parole, sort of.

I waited for who the fuck knows how long, but I wasn't going to wait for whoever it was. Fuckin' A. I could've imagined it. I sure's hell wasn't gonna stick around.

I climbed out the window. It slid open real easy and man I gotta tell you the air on the outside was hot and thick. I felt like I took a lungful of mayonnaise, or a Pall Mall straight. Once the spots cleared and the lightheadedness passed I found some kind of trellis and climbed down.

Damn that was some crib. We're talkin' mansion here, and it took me some acrobatics to negotiate the stone ledges and wooden shutters that were covered with fancy vines. Now we're not talkin' cheapo stuff here, these were fancy landscaped designer plants I was clingin' to made to be just so, to show off the house. When I finally touched ground on the first floor and took a few steps I looked it over. I couldn't take in the whole pad, or the extent of how huge the joint was. I had the heebie-jeebies. Needed another pop.

Whatever this place was once, it wasn't gonna be around much longer, and either was I. Maybe they'd turned an old house into hotel--fuck it--who knows? If it was a hotel it'd probably cost more to stay there for a night than the sticker price of my car in the showroom--which incidentally--I started to get edgy wondering where the fuck it was. I started to freak, and went looking for it I had enough of this flippy zone.

Once I adjusted myself to being on the grass, scoping out the digs, I figured there had to be a parking zone, maybe a row of garages that big pads like this do. Maybe even stables to keep thoroughbreds, Polo Ponies, or Dressage Horses. Whoever owned this place had some serious bank, and with my scattered state of mind wasn't in any shape to scope out how much or how I could put some of that into some of my pile. No way of moving any chips across the table today. I had to bolt. Too much to figure out. But bet your ass I was makin' some mental notes on where things were for the time, which might come sooner or later for me to make some bank. And then things went to shit.

Dogs.

17

Woof Woof Get off My Ass

I hate guard dogs, and the only thing I hate more than guard dogs are a lot of guard dogs. The next notch up is the guy with the shotgun who tends to the fucking beasts. And there they were maybe four or five of them, Dobermans, barking like they haven't eaten in months, or were woken up and told to go fuck with someone. Today that someone was me Neal Grinder. A barefoot motherfucker.

They were coming from all directions, and I didn't know what the fuck to do. Usually I can get out of a jam, but this one was gonna end with some ripped flesh if some miracle didn't fall out of the sky and that wasn't gonna happen. I busted into a run toward what looked like the servant's quarters. Why? It looked unkempt, like an unshaven pussy on a good looking broad. Everything's tip top and classy above the waist, but under that skirt or slacks is some serious Feminist Fallopian foliage. Pubes going every which way but neat. The neglected zone meant a place used mainly for utilitarian purposes hence, the dumpiest foul smelling part of the grounds. It wasn't hard to find because that's where I first saw the trash cans. I knew I was onto something when I saw a clothesline and some sheets hanging. About as out of place at this estate as a Cartier shop next to a trailer park.

Badabing. I knew where they kept the things that'd be an eyesore, and that's where I was headed. A dog came out of nowhere, leapt hard and fast its mouth open and my arm between it's tongue and teeth. I kicked the mutt hard, and it slipped off my leather coat-the motherfucker put a gash in my jacket, but my arm was OK.

I picked up my pace and saw a row of hedges between me the mutts and the slave's hut-and there it was. A row of garage doors, a Bentley, a pair of Ferraris, a Rolls, a Porsche, and you got it baby, my Caddy. The top down and at the end of the driveway as if it'd been parked half-assed by some bimmy who didn't give a shit. The top was down and just as a pair of Doberman's got over the hedges I was in the driver's seat my fingers tickling the keys that were in the ignition. That baby roared to life and I peeled rubber on the high falutin cobblestone drive onto the street, and gunned it. Marone! I wiped the sweat from my upper lip, and forehead, reached into the glove box and grabbed a smoke I'm gonna quit soon, but not today. Damn I'm sure glad I keep an extra pair of shit kickers in the trunk, you never know when you might get stuck in the mud, and baby I was in some serious mud. Where the fuck was I?

Wherever I was, I needed a drink and had to get someplace where I belong like the other side of the tracks.

I was wondering where CP was.

18

CP AWAKES TO HIS OLD DIGS IN 2013
BACK TO WHERE I WAS SOMEHOW

I awoke again. What the fuck. Was this going to be another weird dream? I heard sounds of automobile horns, road rage curses, and cars rumbling over the metal and concrete drawbridge above me. I knew that--but didn't know how I knew it--I was flat on my back staring up at the underside of the bridge, a bridge I'd known. I'm fuzzy headed like I'd had too much cheap wine with a hint, but not much memory of the day before. I had some bizarre dreams. Could I be in another one of them now? They say you can't smell things in your dreams, or you can't write anything down. My notebook was next to me so I grabbed it and went looking for something to write with. I write down my dreams because they must mean something. I began to scrawl, something was wrong. The pen. I'd never seen it before. It was an odd writing instrument a Mont Blanc sort of job only the

star at its end was made of an amber colored crystal--
like a gemstone.

I am certain that more happened yesterday than that
dream. Last night I fell asleep in a beautiful home by
the sea with a beautiful woman, and it smelled great. I
must have dreamt I'd awoken in the year 2070 in a
nice joint, the ocean nearby, and on some sort of
estate, and then passed out.

Today I smell garbage, hear the voices of belligerent
winos, and the street chatter of drug dealers hustling
one thing or another. I looked up, and saw the bottom
of a metal drawbridge, and the occasional clackety
clack of cars heading into the city. Big Town. I was
home--or what had been my home for the last few
months under a bridge in a crummy part of a city.
Something about it doesn't look as familiar as it did--
something's changed, maybe it's me, but it's not as I
recall it. I've changed. I look around and feel a vitality
that'd been gone ten, maybe twenty years ago. There's
something astir and there are parts of me that ache
that I forgot I still had.

I look around, sure I've been here before, but I was
somewhere else for a while. Was it all a dream? I look
at my hands, my fingernails were manicured. Shit.
My fingers look younger as if years of hard living had
been reversed. Then again, was there any hard living--
what happened to me? Something happened--It was
like a dream, and this wasn't. I was in some sort of
nightmare, and I knew I wasn't dreaming because I
could feel the stubble on my face, and smell the coffee

wafting up from the street. I rubbed my face and slowly fragments of memories emerged.

Where is the beautiful home? Where is that large automobile. And where the fuck is that beautiful woman? Questions, questions questions. Here I am in the slums of Big Town, under the bridge I lived at yesterday--if there even was a yesterday that still existed on a space-time continuum--did it? Where's anyone familiar? Nell, the hooker is still on the street. I knew that the blonde wig covered the street walker's natural afro. She was working she said, through law school yeah, right. What law was that? I laughed to myself, and I'm a doctor too.

I stopped midway to the street. Something struck me like a stomach cramp, and I needed a toilet. I ran up to my grocery cart, pulled out some papers, and found my stash, that's where I kept important stuff. Shit, I am a doctor. I realized how much I knew, and that I lived under a bridge because of one out of a few ex-wives, a handful of malpractice suits, and a general distaste for the straight world. I was by my own choosing, a bum. That worked. I was feeling better already when I got to the street.

The convenience store is still there--a joint run by third world folks that catered to the street people--I'm sure they'd have a newspaper and some Joe. I left my shopping cart in place. Stuffed some stuff in my pockets, a bank card, some cash, my spare wallet, I didn't know where my usual one was. The threads I wore had empty pockets, just the pen. Fine. I walk down the concrete embankment beneath the bridge and breathe in the morning stench. Trash collectors don't make usual collections in this part of town--I knew that--chalk that up for a shard of memory. Maybe more would come back as I got my blood flowing. I looked around.

The outlines of my reality were taking shape, and like a half-ass coloring book for the color-blind, there were the gaps. My mind began filling in the spaces with the leftover crayons of my mind. Colors nobody would use they'd be too grim. The old mom and pop businesses were boarded up. A crooked chiropractor shared an office with a few other doctors seemed, like it was in business. The massage parlor next door looked as busy as the shot and a beer bar with the neon pink light in the sole window simply said: "L I Q U O R" -- must have gone kablooey somewhere in the last decade, and the bar's owner, Zill Crapmonger--damn

I knew the slum lord's name, he was too cheap to fix it. There was some religious outpost that said they saved souls. I couldn't recall that joint on account there weren't many souls worth saving in this part of the world. It was desperation alley and the smell of faded dreams stunk like cheap booze, cigarettes, reefer, and Nell's perfume.

Shit, the two story strip must have been one of modern urban development's first strip malls. If you would have asked me then how I knew what I knew, I'd have drawn a blank. But that was then. I needed to snag some java and find a computer. I had one, had it forever, but to be safe brought along the battery pack to swipe a charge at the convenience store.

I greeted the joints owner, an Asian fellow with a comb over. A turban would have been more becoming, but hey, how do you tell a guy he looks like shit when you look shittier? He acted like I was a long lost cousin, maybe it was the cash I laid on the counter, or my radiant charm. Maybe it was the overpriced six pack of extra-proof beer. It didn't occur to me that I was wearing a high end suit of clothes until Nell pointed it out as I sat sipping coffee, waiting for my computer to charge.

I chased a ten milligram Percodan down with some tepid stale coffee and watched old time comedians on Youtube. Facebook, now that I know what it is, a repository for bill collectors, is off limits. The facial recog software has gotten so slick they can track a scofflaw like yours truly faster than you can say what the fuck? And that's pretty much what I had to say.

"Whass with you?" Nell had come over to where I was sitting, my back to the wall of the store facing the parking lot. "You gots a light CP?"

"Want a beer?" I held out a can."

"Sure, sugah," she said.

I cracked open the flip top and handed it to her before setting into my tale. "I went to sleep last night next to a beautiful woman in an ornate bedroom in a mansion by the sea. Dreamed strange dreams and awoke as I often do, under a bridge shivering in a raggedy sleeping bag."

"Yeah, sure you did," she leaned over hiking up her miniskirt to reveal a clean shaven nether zone, that'd seen more traffic in a night than the main drag in this part of town sees in a year.

"Yeah, sure Nell." I took out a book of matches. I'd swiped them from store because I knew that Nell was going to ask me for a light. What the fuck?. Somehow I had some sort of prescience, that I could either see something happen before it did, or I could read minds. I lit her cigarette.

She took a drag of her cigarette, and looked me over. "You okay?"

I had to think. At least my shopping cart was still there and all the shit in it was intact. Big whoop. I pulled one of my hands across my face, dragged it down and shook my head. "I have no idea what happened yesterday."

"I feel dat way every day CP, whass the big deal?"

"I was with a woman," I said.

"You was with that other doctor friend of yours--the one look like he wanna be Elvis, talk like some kinda hoodlum. Grinder. Thass his name, Neal Grinder MD, he a bum like you. Ain't no work for doctor's no more unless they sellin' pills like Zill over there," she pointed her chin to the shabby office between the bar and massage parlor. "Thass my competition them Vietnamese ho's got a massage license too."

I looked over at the office, then Nell. She was smoking, tapping her whore shoes, must have shopped at sluts are us. Full Lucite pumps that gave her an extra three inches in height.

"Wha you lookin' at Doc?"

"Sorry Nell, I'm just a little fuzzy."

"Thass fo sure. You muss got no sleep--Go on up to your digs and crash for a while."

It sounded like a good idea. I poured out what remained of the coffee, and climbed back up to my nest. I had to sort things out--I'd been through something--something as off as I was--a fucking MD, a surgeon, war vet, someone who'd had it all, now living under a bridge.

I put my head back down on the rocks I used as a pillow and stared up at the bottom of the drawbridge that leads into Big Town. Same shit. Noisy cars going to and from the city chasing some long gone American Dream. At least waking up to few pills made the transition from a dream state to this crap more tolerable. I can thank my old pal Grinder for that. He's a scumbag doctor who dabbles in all sorts of unwholesomeness. Yeah, I can see the dreams fade as the outlines of reality got thicker and wondered what happens when you die. Do all the things you've done in your life fade like dreams as the urge to piss mounts and the blaring realities of humanity kick in? I don't know, I've never been dead, but sure have come close. And I know something's about to happen--it's unclear in my mind's eye, maybe it was the Percodan--I'm at a point where I don't know what's real and what's part of a dream, the drugs, or who the fuck knew? It all started with a stupid trip to a clinic yesterday, that much I knew and Nell confirmed it.

What happened next must have been a dream, but I smelled my upper lip it was a woman's scent. It was real, it wasn't going to go away if I stopped believing in it. I wasn't hallucinating. I had no voices talking to me, but I did hear other people's thoughts. Something about me was altered, and it wasn't just the drugs and booze. Damn, I cracked open a beer and looked around. I couldn't shake this sense of impending . . . something. I couldn't put my mind on it but it was going to go down soon. Shit. I popped another pill.

So I'm propped up on my elbows listening to Nell the whore's thoughts, waiting for the drugs to kick in when a car pulls up and a raunchy looking creep with a reddish Kangol hat jumps out and starts to yank at Nell's upper arm. What the fuck? I can hear her thinking . . . no shouting at the guy. I vector in on his head and he's thinking out some weird language but sense that he's got some real meanness. I run down the embankment to break it up. Why? I don't know, I don't like seeing a broad, I don't care if she's a ho or whatever being fucked with. This guy was trouble, and I had the equipment to deal with it. Don't ask me how or why, I just did. Maybe the thousands of back alley scuffles, bar room brawls, battlefields, operating rooms, or tight jams I've been in, I knew that I was capable of damaging this little creep. Maybe five foot six or seven to my six feet buck sixty pounds, but the little monkey looked wiry and mean, and now he had a blade out. What the fuck?

I remembered one thing and don't ask me how or why but put him down fast and ask questions later. I was curious to see if I could get any English out of him. Maybe it was the Percodan or just plain curiosity, but not being able to read his thoughts in a language that made sense was compelling enough to hustle over to the scene. She was already being ushered into the car when I kicked the back of his right knee hard with my heel and brought my elbow down on his right clavicle and heard it snap. He yelped and rolled onto the pavement just as the driver of the car got out, pointed his gun at me, and said: "Freeze gringo!"

At that, Nell had reached into her whore pouch and had a tiny pistol in her hand, she fired once, twice, and we stood side by side as the spic slid down the side of the car. There was the sound of sirens in the air, and this wasn't a place to be when the cops showed up. I looked at Nell and she must have known the same and we ducked into the alley. The punk on the ground with the broken shoulder bone was staring at us as we left. I may not have known what he was saying earlier, but I did now: "I'm gonna get you mother fucker."

There were a few winos looming about who may have been witnesses but wouldn't say a word to a cop. They watched the whole scene go down but watched the shooters leave. One of the winos would later recall that the guy with the bum shoulder was heading toward the shopping cart where CP kept his stuff, but had to skip it when the sirens sounded like they were nearly on the scene. Yeah, they were looking for something.

Herman Duss was seated behind the wheel of a car parked up the street, grinning.

19

2070
THE CHICK FROM THE SACK: NADINE

I woke up alone. The man I shared the bed with was gone, but the impression of his body remained. Was this happening? I pulled up the sheet and looked at my toes, the bed's edge, and beyond to the window and day's light. A storm was approaching. The sky had a yellowish tinge, and distant thunder rumbled. Should I get up and close the window? I'd leave my empty bed--I still smelled him--I wanted him. I ached to be filled and didn't want to leave this warm place. I didn't want to move. He was gone, probably snapped into the space-time continuum. At first I thought it was something I did or said back when we were in another time. No, that wasn't possible, but if I did that may have altered today. Was I all right. Had I changed? I felt my own breast, firm, warm and the shape of a twenty seven year old woman. But my hand seemed to pass across my flesh oddly as if my senses had been altered, numb, not all there. I let my hand roam down, and wondered. How could this have happened, whatever THIS is? Where did he go? The sound of distant thunder sounded like canons, but there were no weapons of that sort in this time--the cannonade came again. I had to move, but I was cold, very cold. I tucked the covers under my chin, and stared at the walls eerily casting long shadows foretelling something beyond my knowing. I needed to know what happened to CP, what was happening to me? Did he have a choice . . . do I?

I tried consoling myself with whatever thoughts came: A good man is hard to find, and a hard man is good to find--but it wasn't amusing. I did have a good man, and now he's gone. My thoughts wandered as the shadows grew. How many times have I been asked what constitutes a good man, and recall how he answered:

"A good car lets you think you're in control. You are to an extent, but a good man will let you know that you are," she said beginning to feel the top of the neatly trimmed pelt at her crotch, and it too was tingling with some static electricity, paresthesias, but why? How?

There was a gentle tap, could it be him? No. Something happened that's taken him away. Something made him disappear, something not of this time and not of his volition. There it is again at the door, and I shout out: "What do you want?"

A huge outline of a person stood in the doorway outlined by the morning light. A man who smelled of creosol, burnt plastic, and spoke with a voice that was deep and sounded like it came from the bottom of a barrel.

"Nadine," the man said. "He's not the one who's gone. Nadine. You didn't let him go, it's you who will not be. Go on, look at yourself. You're fading, and before long, you will have never been."

I looked at my hand, what the hell? I dropped the blankets, I didn't care if he saw me, if he saw me, my hand was becoming transparent as we spoke. I grabbed myself, and felt myself dwindle as though I was ceasing to exist.

"Who are you?"

"You know me, Nadine. You know me from 1958, and all ten toes were very real.

Now get up and help me find him. He's taken something that doesn't belong to him."

20

2013 CP, Nell, The Bad Guys, And Stale Coffee

CP and Nell watched from the alley they had ducked into as the cop cars rolled by, decided anything can happen in this crappy part of town and usually does. Rolled past the scene of what may have been a crime, but decided it was just another slum drug deal gone bad, and peeled rubber out of that crummy part of town.

"Who were those guys, Nell?"

"I ain't never seen `em."

"You sure you didn't piss off some Johns?"

"Hell no CP, I never piss off but nobody. Them was Latinos and I don't do no bidnet with no cha cha cha gang bangers. Beside, they don't likes the brown sugar."

"I need some coffee let's go over to Buckaroo Bagwams."

Bagwam's was the convenience store that sold cheap booze and smokes to the bums and beggars at above market price and kept a stack of old newspapers for any passerby who might get lost-which were few. Nobody from the straight world showed up in this side of the city, and if they did they might live to regret it.

Tires squealed and CP craned his neck, Nell the ho said: "Shit they's back."

Three gunshots.

Bang, pause. Bang Bang.

"Shit. These sound almost like pros." CP said aloud, and grabbed Nell ducking behind a parked car. The rear window shattered, glass projectiles sprayed the sidewalk. The winos looming scattered. Shit. What the hell is this all about?

Just then a red pickup truck pulled up and hopped the curb. A man in a ratty straw cowboy hat, sunglasses, and a bandana covering his face leaned over and shoved open the passenger door.

"Hey ya'all, get in!" The driver had a thick drawl in the you all.

Nell saw the open door and may have thought it was a quick trick to turn. She shrugged, poofed her hair extensions, and looked over at CP before heading toward the truck at a double time pace.

CP looked at Nell, shook his head and thought, dumb ho. Then took a gander at the guy behind the wheel. He had on beat up jeans, a calico shirt and didn't look like he'd ventured far off of a farm, but the nearest farmland was miles and miles away from Big Town's notorious seedier side of the tracks. "How do I know you're not some crumb like those assholes that spit bullets and got Nell riled?"

"Trust me pal, I ain't no criminal. Them muggers t'weren't no muggers at all, they wanted somethin' from you and grabbed the colored gal to misdirect you," he said.

Nell the hooker already got on board and slid toward the hick.

"What did they want?" CP knew that getting in the truck was the easiest route to take but something was just off kilter today. Shit. What the fuck happened to yesterday? He thought as he put one foot in front of the other toward the rickety flatbed gas guzzling heap of hillbilly highway junk. Shit, this asshole better know what the deal is. "You are going to explain this aren't you?"

"Get the heck in and I'll tell ya." The hick waved his arm hard and fast. "C'mon you never know who's gonna show up next, or for what. We're all in danger. Grave danger!"

"As if there's any other kind," CP said plopping himself on the bench seat next to Nell, who'd already made herself comfy. Dumb ho. She'll get in a vehicle with the devil himself.

"Who the fuck are you?" CP said.

"Well howdy doody friends, my name's Eustice. Eustice Seeney, and I'm at your service." The driver said.

He kept his head facing forward, and spoke in that accent reserved for airboat tour guides, inbred hillbillies with six fingers, and people who guard stills with sawed off shotguns. Or so CP would later recall.

"What are you? Some kinda Duke of Hazzard Jethro?" Nell the hooker had her balled up hands on her hips.

She spoke in a tone of authority--more cop than crook--somewhat off for a street ho. Nasty--CP thought--would be more appropriate of her actual station in life. Everything seemed to CP somewhat off kilter, not anything he could put his finger on. Just the subtleness of things wasn't as it should be. He looked at Nell, and reconsidered.

She hadn't always trolled the avenue of the inner city selling sex to passerby horn dogs, she was actually employed . . but that's another story.

Nell's business turning tricks in the slum where CP lived, across from the overpriced convenience store wasn't exactly going to be in a taxable income bracket either.

Nell, upon reflection couldn't recall the last customer she'd had, and to those ends she'd become concerned that her fellatial skills may be lacking. She eyed the masked man driving the pickup truck with the sort of curious gaze a hungry animal might have.

"Nah," she said: "Where you takin' us hillbilly man?"

"I'm rescuin' you from the time bandits."

"Say what?" Nell said.

"Them folks swooped on over to get what's in that shoppin' cart. Ain't no way that can happen. That can't see the light of day. Nope, that can't happen on account them's is bad folks lookin' to take stuff. I can't let it fall into THEIR evil hands."

"And what might that be, Eustice?" CP asked.

"Well you got yourself a metronomic capitulator that plucks out mymine chips that've been implanted in people. It looks like a notebook computer but it ain't."

"Say what hillbilly?" Nell swatted her hand like an insect was buzzing around her tits. "Metronomic capisshillator?"

"Yep, that's what it is." The Hillbilly said.

"What the hell's that motherfuckin' thing, and why them Latinos wanna shoot me and CP for it?"

"Ma'am, thass an interestin' question, but I'm gonna have to let the doc `splain that to you."

"Doc?" CP said. "What doctor are you talking about?"

"I ain't s'posed to say but for nothin'. I juss got sent here to run a errand, thass it."

"Sheeyatt, you redneck. What the motherfuckin' shit you good for? Huh?"

"I got me a pint of Early Times in the glove box." The driver notched his head in the direction in front of CPs knees. "Go on help yourself."

"Now you talkin'," she said reaching for the bottle.

21

2013
Grinder Goes for Drinks Across the Tracks

The joint sat with pride of purpose in a gravel parking lot surrounded by a chain link fence. There was a mobile home park next door with an abandoned guardhouse. A kids playground, set, that judging by the empty bottles, cans, and cigarette butts probably saw more stoners, winos, and bums than kids riding the off kilter see saw.

The convenience store across the street had signs on the windows that you could pick up lottery tickets, cheap beer, and smokes, and that the place was under twenty-four hour surveillance. Yeah right.

There was an unoccupied chiropractor's office. You could tell by the rickety sign hanging askew above the door. And the heap of plastic wrapped newspapers, which upon inspection a straggler would notice the dates being a few months old. All this was on the east side of of the railroad tracks just outside of Boca Raton, Florida.

The stand alone bar was a cinder block one story shabby little shot and a beer joint with tinted glass windows displaying one or another brand of liquor, and a sign that had been changed as many times as owners. A reasonable assessment by a sober passerby was that it'd been in foreclosure a few times because of the fragments of eviction notices stuck to the door.

Tax liens have an official look and the type of adhesive that doesn't wash off in the rain. Pair that up with the flickering name of the place: "Joes First Class Bar" and you get the sense that Joe was on the lam and the place catered to a handful of regulars none of which ever having flown business, let alone that lofty comfort of a jetliner. The dump, most folks in the know knew, had changed ownership more often than a guy with half his intestines. Take a few bites of fried calamari and chase it with a watered down brew.

Many shops, offices, and restaurants have a bell or buzzer that signals entry or exit of clients. Joe's had the "Doink Doink" sound from the TV Show, "Law and Order" when someone opened the door.

"Poop" sat on a barstool drinking a beer from a frosty mug. There was an untouched shot glass on a napkin waiting to be in the company of the three other shot glasses-the empty ones-six inches away. Poop was half in the bag, the other half was telling tall tales that the bartender, a fiftyish woman who'd heard them again and again just rolled her eyes.

Maxine Pearlmutter tended bar to make ends meet knowing of course that they never would. At least the liquor was one part of the job that made life tolerable. Sitting at home in her beat up fake leather chair, propped on pillows, watching reruns of : My Name is Earl, Jerry Springer, and the Cooking Channel cost money. Money for the cable TV bill, and her ex husband, who'd been crashing at the trailer hadn't seen sobriety in six years. Since the last wave of the great recession washed his career dreams down the tubes. So much for work as a security guard. So she took the job at the bar, on the other side of the chain link fence surrounding their home at the trailer park.

The neighbors were friendly enough considering they were all casualties of the class wars, and somehow wore their medals of honor in not so mobile mobile homes. The unemployment rate was somewhere near ninety nine percent, and anyone not collecting public assistance was suspect. After all, who knew or trusted a "stranger" NOT receiving a li'l help from Uncle Sammy, right? Maxine used to be proud, but now she knew that drunk was better.

"Hey Poop, are you gonna drink that drink or just talk about the good old days?" She said knowing he probably couldn't hear a word of what she said .

There was some background music the guy shooting billiards had cranked up. She hadn't seen the guy in here before, but any face other than Poop's was the possibility of a tip, and she did notice the red Cadillac convertible he had in the lot.

"Do you know who I am?" Poop started to stand up. He had the shot glass in his hand, and was talking to the guy shooting pool, who proceeded to ignore the gremlin like man at the bar.

Maxine noticed the guy with the pool cue had perfectly manicured mutton chop sideburns trimmed to Elvis style perfection, and thinning hair to match. He wore a thin leather jacket, which was unusual for South Florida, but hey people paying their bill could dress however they wanted, and Elvis over there slapped a C note on the bar, asked for a pack of Marlboro's and a pitcher, so fuck the dress code. Not that there really was one other than shoes and a shirt. After all it was Florida.

"Hey buddy I'll shoot a game of pool wiff you," Poop said. "But I gotta take a shit first. I had my bowels operated on you know?"

"Shut up and drink your drink Poop, can't you see the man's busy."

"Nobody's show busy they don't have time for me." Poop said downing his shot of Old Crud and saying, "I'll be right back I gotta take a shit. Don't fuck with me when I'm shitting. I gotta gun, See." Poop patted his side. "Walther PPK, juss like 007, I'm ready for anything. Spades, spics, guineas, you name it. Don't diss me, don't fuck with me."

"Have a nice dump, pal." Grinder said, then looked at the barmaid.

Ten minutes of old 50s music later Poop reappeared zipping up his trousers, and said to the man shooting pool, "Wash your deal?"

"You talkin' to me?" The guy at the pool table held his stick like a rifle and lowered his sunglasses.

"Yesh I am tarking to you." Poop slurred.

"Sit down Poop you're scaring away the customers."

"Aye, it's okay lady, the old drunk needs some conversation. No big deal."

"Are you sure, sir?"

The man started into a lecture to Maxine and Poop and this is what he said:

"So I'm minding my business doin' what I dig, which is usually watchin' some slutty hos, sippin' a brew or three, shootin' pool, and hangin' with a few bros. Yeah yeah I'm gettin' too old to be irresponsible and should be doin' righteous shit and all, but you know what? I already took that route, played by the rules of society, did all the politically correct shit, and where'd it get me? Where'd it get anyone? We got a country goin' down the friggin' crapper, news pundits bullshitting one thing or another gettin' dummies dumb enough to listen all riled up, and a handful of mini wars popping up so fast I quit counting. The muzzies are on a rampage because some joker made a movie about their religion they didn't like and decided to jack everyone off. The queers have gone apeshit over some guy--an owner of a restaurant chain--said out loud what he thought, that homos shouldn't be getting married, and the world of nicey nice phony baloney non GMO eating, vegan and granola types flipped out. A little while ago some colored kid in a gangsta get up gets himself shot for being at some ritzy place-as if that sort of crap doesn't happen all the time, and the country shuts down. Don't get me started on politics wait, I already did get started. The stupid election. It ain't about politics, no way, never was. Black president and the whole country who secretly still calls black people coloreds goes apeshit-not politically correct, right?"

"Right."

"The election isn't about any agenda, the economy, the banks that've been ripping people off, hell no! This shit is about the color of the guys skin, nothing else. Granted blacks in the US have had a bum rap, but so've the spics, Jews, Micks, you name it the minority is always in the minority."

"I may be a little buzzed but I think that makes sense, right?"

"Hell yes. There just so happens to be a lot more blacks, and now the store managers, clerks, and whole kit and caboodle have come out to mark their new territory like they own US. Just like the colored folks do at the DMV. That's right the whole friggin' country's turned into one big driver's license renewal center with a big smiling picture of the president. And the clerks giving you shit about not having one document or another, have a whole new set of privileges to jerk us around in the: 'See that man on the wall? Take a look at his picture, he's on OUR side.' And then THEY-the colored people go about their business telling you to go to the back of the line blah blah blah. As if American's are really up for the whole fried chicken and biscuit eating, high jumping, slam dunking, set to give THEM orders . . . But that's been happening. The American empowerment of Negroes. The confidence to tell whitey to shut the fuck up, all that and a whole lot more. And then they go on their break. I'll have another beer." He finally stopped talking and hollered to the bar tender.

"That was a good rap. Hold on I gotta take a shit," Poop said.

"You just did." The man said.

"He's only got half his guts," Maxine said.

"Fuckin' A, man. Fuckin' A."

The phone rang. Maxine answered it and yelled out: "You Grinder?"

"Yeah."

"It's for you." She plopped the telephone on the bar, and held up the handpiece. "C'mon I ain't got all day."

Grinder took the call

Less than five minutes later, he dropped the phone, and ran out of the bar.

"Hey you didn't pay your tab!"

Grinder didn't hear her, or care. He was already revving the Cadillac's engine and didn't notice Poop had followed him out, his hand at his side.

22

BACK IN THE TRUCK

The guy in the straw cowboy hat, bandana face mask, and shades wearing beat up jeans and a calico shirt was focused on driving the pickup truck. CP was leaning down, looking at the side view mirror, and Nell sat in the center of the truck's bench seat. Every time the driver changed gears the transmission growled, crunched, and made noises like the rickety ride was going to fall apart the next time it slipped into gear, but it didn't. He sped off, leaving whatever was going on back there in the distance.

"You some guardian angel, superhero, or concerned citizen?" CP said over the noises of the decades old truck which he would later recall had a real nasty paint job, as if it had been touched up a few times too many by idiots on acid, alcohol, or some other mind altering drugs.

"Yeah, who you am?" Nell said, fixing herself up, staring into the rearview mirror at her smudged lipstick, and then fussing with the hair extensions.

"You two's real lucky today," the driver said.

"Lucky?" CP said arching an eyebrow, leaning over Nell's lap. "Who the fuck are you and what's your deal. You look like you just left farm country?"

"Hold your horses there fella. My name's Eustice, and I just saved you two from the minions of Satan. Them folks shootin' at you din't care iffen you got dead or not, they wanted somethin' you Mr. CP got, and was gonna do whatever it takes to get it."

"How you know CP's name hillbilly boy?" Nell said.

"Yeah, how do you know this shit? Who are you?"

Changing gears again, and slowing down, the driver said: "Mah name's Eustice Seeney, and I ain't from these parts, in fack I come from a whole different place. But that ain't got no matter on the grounds that I have been dead, come back to life, and know as a fact that some sinister forces is gonna be where they is when they is, and my job is to find out what they're up to, and stop em from gettin' their way. I'm on a mission."

"A mission? What're you an evangelist, or some Hari Krishna washout?"

"Yeah. What you is, some kinda freak?"

"No ma'am. I died, went to hell, and came back. I found out that the devil controls lots of stuff here. This is gonna sound strange to you, and ya'all might not believe it, but I travel through time to save folks from eternal damnation and get in the Devil's way so he can't wreck the world."

"And you do this for how much money?" Nell made the universal rolling of her thumb and forefinger of "how much" with her long nailed fingers.

"Ain't got no fee. I'm just in the business of savin' myself from eternal damnation."

"OK buddy." CP said, in that, shit I've had enough craziness for one day tone, "You can drop me off next chance so I can get back to what I don't have to do."

"No can do, son." Eustice said. "I gotta take you to see someone."

"Say what, Jim?" Nell said leaning back looking at the driver in that "who farted" manner people do when they smell something fishy.

"Doc Beaufort wants to see you." Eustice said.

Something rang a bell or hit a chime because CP had some sort of an ah-ha moment, his face dropped a few shades to ghost-like pale, and he felt shaky. He knew Beaufort, but for some reason he couldn't access those memories. It was as if he knew what the color yellow was, but couldn't visualize it. This is the first time CP could remember that his brain could work in such a way. It freaked him out. "I know that name, Beaufort, but I don't know how or why."

The driver said: "Ah know that, and ole Doc Beaufort said that he knew you'd be all freaked out like you is, so set back and enjoy the ride. We're gonna take a trip and you'll learn the whole shebang."

"Where we goin' hillbilly boy?" Nell said, lighting up a cigarette.

"I'd rather you not smoke right now ma'am, we're going to be driving from 2013 to 1958, and on the way that cigarette smoke could throw things off and land us someplace in between. I don't right know about you but sure's hell don't wanna get stuck in the 90s."

"Say what?"

"The radio," Eustice tapped the radio of the truck. "That there tells me where I'm at, and I swear if I gotta hear Vanilla Ice one more time I'll have a seizure."

"Okay okay, honky." She put away the cigarette.

"This is insane," CP said. "Not because it seems that way on the surface, but because I know what you're saying and it isn't bullshit, but somehow the memories of why it should make sense are gone. You showing up make perfectly good sense on some level, I just can't access that part of my mind that understands it."

"Don't worry friend. Like I said the Doc will explain all that to you, so buckle up."

23

NADINE

I was born in 2040, and shortly after birth my DNA was modified to prevent any mutations that might cause what remained from the wars. When I turned twenty-five or so I had to leave my job at the time travel historical documentation center because I accidentally let the past enter the future and return without erasing their memory. In doing so it caused a time paradox which altered, ever so slightly, yet significantly enough to be punished.

Let me tell you how fascinating it was to help people living in the miserable year 2070. The times were truly vapid. Nothing was going on other than constant surveillance by the government, little to do for entertainment, and horrible food. The earth had become infested with disease free, and quarantine zones. The disease free zones were inhabited largely by the extremely affluent-mostly old families from around the world. The quarantine zones were my worst nightmare. Those were areas where the desperate roamed, mutants, cripples, emotionally unhinged, and those whose bodies could not for one biochemical reason or another accept the mymine chips. Their bodies rejected the cyclic nucleotide as a foreign object, and they became violently ill. Many became mad, and went on some sort of rampage or another. Criminals actually, and had to be restricted from the larger society. In fact those of us living in safe zones were always on the lookout for a Quarntos who'd managed to escape and infiltrate the disease free zones. The world was divided into the Disease Free Zones and the Q Zones.

Being born into a Difree Zone and studying the history of earth before the cell phone wars was my forte before my little incident. Like I said, I brought back a twentieth century person, they saw the future, went back, and began writing stories. Fortunately none of them became popular and the author, a bum of sorts, disappeared. Actually I brought him to the year 2070 to shut him up. Which is where things began to get messy. I will get back to that.

In 2070 the greatest events for the wealthy was to travel through time. The goal ultimately was to settle some place in history and enjoy their lives in a past that wasn't damaged by the mutating winds that engulfed the earth after the cell phone wars. We were essentially always on the lookout for an EM storm that could send your DNA into a frenzy, and shelters of a kind were everywhere. The most common were malls. At the slightest warning that an EM storm was brewing the mall would charge up and surround itself with a repellant shield. Occasionally a criminal from the Quarnto zone would rupture the cover, and the shoppers would become mymine inactivated, rapidly age, and shrivel up and die-it was horrible.

The mymine chip was an addition to our DNA that prevented aging, eliminated disease, and allowed those of us not in a Q zone to use telepathy. If you grew up with it, mind reading, as they called it in the past was nothing special.

The malls themselves were lovely displays of different periods in history where people could step into and visit. As long as the rules were followed everything went well. But things did not always go well because our government was not always on top of the corruption of time travelers. That's why we had the TBI, or Time Bureau of Investigation. They helped keep the organized crime group, the largest of the criminals from causing havoc with those who settled in some part of human history.

People actually went back to Ancient Rome, the Renaissance in Europe, America's Wild West, and countless times and places where innocence truly existed. Of course the bad people wanted to seize what they did not or could not have, and many were defective humans from the Q Zone who were seemingly always trying to make trouble. The gangster operation known as "The Organization" made a pact with our Provisional Government to work together to weed out chip thieves who would travel back in time, and make trouble before their chips were rejected. Unfortunately that didn't always happen, and outposts at different periods were set up. A few good people manned those stations to put a halt to the TI, or Time Interlopers. Thank goodness.

So my punishment was to spend some indeterminable period of time with one of the sentinels at time in history that was quite peaceful, and also a very desirable location for scoundrels to visit.

I was sent to live with a nice couple in the year 1958, to assist Doc Beaufort and Milly in preventing any space-time continuum irregularities from becoming future historical waves, or EM bursts from occurring. It was quite a job.

The government was provisional because the times were always changing.

24

BACK IN THE TRUCK'S CAB

"This here's the deal," the hick started to say. "We gotta make a time leap."

"What the fuck you talkin' bout hillbilly boy?" Nell the ho said more than asked, and took a long pull from the pint bottle of Early Times the driver offered.

"Time leap? Yeah, right." CP said. "I suppose we're going to the future." Glibly studying the bottle then putting it in the glove box thinking he'd rather not be fucked up for this. "So where are we leaping to?"

"Hells fire we's goin' to nineteen fifty eight." The masked man said.

CP could almost see him smiling beneath the bandana. "How the hell are we going to do that?"

"We's gotta get out to the country and find us a cornfield."

"You crazy, hillbilly boy." Nell said. "Why we gotta do dat?"

"Mebbe so, but that metronomic capitulator that them guys was lookin' for may already be in use by them bad guys. So hang on."

He was weaving in and out of traffic, speeding, and to a police cruiser might have been easy pickings. To a road rager, a target.

"Maybe you ought to take it easy," CP said.

"I ain't worried but for nothin', " Eustice said. "We're protected." He turned the knob of the radio hard right filling the cabin with the pulsating bass of hip hop music, and then pointed to the sky. "Yep, we's beein' looked after."

At that, a car pulled up alongside the truck, rolled down the driver's side window and some guy started hollering.

"Shit Seeney, that guy probably has a gun!" CP said. "You cut him off in traffic, man."

Seeney gunned the engine, downshifted, and sped past the angry motorist.

"We got us an appointment with history." Eustice said.

"Yeah, right." CP said blowing a lungful of air out through his clenched teeth.

"Sheeyatt somebody does."

25

AN APPOINTMENT WITH HISTORY

Two Goofballs and the Metronomic Capitulator

"My focking shoulder hurts, meng." Alejandro Barcado said from the passenger seat rubbing himself with one hand, and fiddling with the fuzzy dice dangling from the rearview mirror.

"Shut up Alejandro. You did get the thing, didn't you, man?" Bart Pinto was driving. He'd had enough of this idiot already. Nothing but dead weight with a busted shoulder bone.

"Chit yeah," he said dropping his hand and lifting the notebook size box off the passenger side floor of the car.

"That fucking hat looks stupid Alejandro." Bart said. "Whoever saw that go down is going to remember that."

"Hey meng, thass my badass hat." He put the device back on the floor and adjusted his hat. "This is cool, meng."

"Cool my ass. It'll be real cool when you're sitting in front of a judge. You know they make you take your hat off in the courtroom."

"Who says nothin' about no courtroom?"

"Just shut the fuck up."

"Fock you, Pinto. We in diss together and lass time I looked we got the same boss."

"Yeah, well if we get pinched the Cobbler will have both of us killed."

"We ain't gettin' pinched. We're deliverin' meng. We got de stoff, and dats our focking job, meng."

"Didn't I tell you to shut the fuck up?"

They got on the expressway and headed away from the city. The dense cloud cover began to thin out, going from a dirty darkness of industrialization, pollution, and smog, to a wispy gloom, finally giving way to a blueness tattered with wispy clouds.

"This is some nice shit, man," Alejandro said.

"I told you to shut up."

The two men didn't speak as they rode out of the labyrinth of familiar streets.

They both were aware of how the traffic thinned as they got farther from Big Town.

When they were deep into the countryside surrounded by farmland Bart Pinto said: "Here's the exit the man told us about. Get that thing ready."

"Cheesh meng, iss ready. Ain't nebber been unready. My focking shoulder hurts and I juss wanna get thiss sheet ober wit."

"Do you ever stop bitching Alejandro? You sound like a little girl?"

"Who ju callin' a leetle girl, huh meng?"

"Do you know how to turn that thing on?" Bart Pinto nudged his head toward the metronomic capitulator at Alejandro's feet.

"You theenk I'm stupeed, no? Iss got a on and off swish see." Alejandro hefted the device up, shoved it in Bart Pinto's face and shook it. "Thiss is eet Peento. You better stop gibbin me cheet meng, or else."

"Or what? You fucking cock blocking douchebag? What the fuck are you going to do? You fuck with me and you'll be back washing dishes at the spico hacienda you came from."

"I'm gonna get disability for my shoulder you focker." Alejandro rubbed his upper torso.

"It's not your shoulder asshole, it's your collar bone, and you ain't getting shit. Just turn the fucking box on." Pinto said.

They were in farm country now. Bart rolled down his window and took a deep breath. "Damn that smells good and fresh."

"Smells like cow sheet." Alejandro said in a sulking tone. "Focking cow sheet."

"Just enjoy being outside of the city you slob. Look at the sky, it's clear and the sun's shining."

"I'll enjoy the money when the man pays us the other half."

"Is that the turn off Alejandro?"

"Turn off? Thass just some dusty unpaved street that goes right into the cornfield, thass what it is."

"That's where we're supposed to take this fucking thing. So hang on you retard."

"Who ju calling a retard? I'd kick you're ass if you wasn't driving."

"Yeah, you ain't doing shit, asshole."

Pinto slowed the car, made the turn and drove into the cornfield. He looked at the map that Herman Duss had given him one more time before folding it and putting it in the glove box. Duss, he patted his pocket, felt the wad of cash. Not a bad score at all. Too bad that jerk Alejandro saw how much it was.

27

CP, Nell, and Eustice in the Pickup Truck to Someplace

I hate fucking loud commercials. Seriously. Living under a bridge and listening to the traffic on the drawbridge is soothing, consistent, and puts me in a Zen like trance. Then again that's a whole different story, I'll get back to it. For now the music was over and some asshole was playing a moronic jingle about this or that, and it was decibels louder than the obnoxious twentieth century music station hillbilly boy was listening to.

"Can you turn the damn radio down please?" I said. My head felt like a platoon of caterpillars in steel toed boots crawled in my skull, and were dancing to Vanilla Ice's tome to hip hop.

"Hey CP. Thass a good station. You go crisizin' people's music? Hellsfire that can get you shot collsarn it." The driver, Eustice, said in no uncertain terms.

"What you gonna do shoot us hillbilly boy?" Nell said.

"Heck no ma'am, I was just sayin'." Eustice said and turned down the volume.

Everyone owns a gun in America and keeps it close by. That is the way you've got to think traveling around the US these days. Americans are at the edge of their conscious seat of sanity, and ready to fly off the handle on a whim. Cut someone off in traffic boom instead of toot, toot, toot. Cross the double yellow line, boom. Not a cop in sight, but a bullet through your window. You look at someone funny you've gotta figure they're gonna put a bullet in you. Why? Why the fuck in the twenty first century do Americans have this simmering craziness and itchy trigger finger sans some internal editor, or mindful inhibitor to make them stop, think, and take a fraction of second to look at the consequences of their actions?

I don't know. Maybe it's the spate of commercials on everything everywhere, that unconsciously triggers some madness like those subliminal ads they used to have in movie theaters to make you crave popcorn.

The US has gotten so hog wild about selling garbage that the advertisers put a commercial plug everywhere, and tweak up the volume on the TV and radio for some nonsense. The internet has bots that read your email electronically, and post pop up ads that drive you and your computer nuts. Youtube, Facebook, Yahoo, you name it-every site has a billion freaking ads you have to sift through to get you to eyeball some garbage the grand marketing machines figured that YOU PERSONALLY NEED.

Now that really sucks rat shit. You fucking hate checking your email because you gotta go through twenty fucking ads and a thousand spammy pieces of crap before you get to it. Jeepers I've won the Nigerian lottery ten times today, and have ads for enough boner medicine to wrap my penis around the world six times-and that's just today. Well I'm not into it. So I guess that mymine chip implanted in my DNA is going to blow .

SHIT. How did I know that?

Yes, bits and pieces of things are coming back to me. I was somehow transported back to the past and then implanted with some cyclic nucleotide that enabled me to read minds.

Son of a bitch. I could read Nell's thoughts as well as those of the crazy driver in the cowboy hat.

What is this weirdo thinking? He's got issues . . . he's got: penile ischemia, anemia, thalassemia, leukemia, bulimia, and hasn't gotten a hard on since the last election. They announced a loss of the election in Japan, and he took it to mean that he would lose his "erection" and had to find a Japanese woman. Or the President of Star Fleet Command would beam him into Jesus Christ's private ante room for a conference with the top Lawyer in hell to negotiate a settlement to end the civil war.

"SHIT STOP THINKING YOU IDIOT" I thought I said to myself but must have blurted it out.

"Hellsfire CP, you can read my mind. I was just thinkin' dopey thoughts to see if you had that special computer chip the Devil puts into people."

"It's not the Devil you moron, it's The Organization, and a doctor that lives in 1958 that inserts them, and it sounds like your chips have gone kablooey." I said.

"Yeah, my thinker brain ain't been workin' right these days. But you only think it's the work of man when it's really supernatural forces." He took his hand off the wheel and pointed to his head like some retard. "The brain gets tricked and it's the work of Satan. Satan's supercomputer is at work, and that Organization is just an extension of the minions of the devil."

"Shit, either way you shake it or bake it Eustice, we have these items--I pointed to my head then his--in our bodies, and from what I gather need servicing."

"What the hell you white boys chatterin' about? I ain't got no shit in mah haid," Nell said searching for a cigarette, and scrunching up her face like both of us were insane. "I needs me another drink." She said.

I handed her the bottle from the glove box: "Listen both of you, my memory's got holes in it, a couple hoods tried to shoot or kidnap Nell, and I have no idea if what happened yesterday was a dream or not."

"Whyzat CP?" Nell took a long pull from the pint bottle. "You wasn't 'round all day, that Elvis lookin' player in the red Cadillac, Grinder, you know the crooked doc in the rag top, came and picked you up early. The guy at the convenience store let me clean up, said you slipped him a few bucks for me. That was nice, I owe you a hand job. I was in there and Bagwam said you and Grinder had some gig out in the boonies."

"Yeah, that's right, we had to do some shit at some clinic and then everything went nuts, we got in an accident, ran into a cornfield, and went back in time. I thought it was a dream."

"Hellsfire, CP, that t'weren't no dream. You really went back in time, and met Doc Beaufort, and that sweet gal Nadine, and then got your ass chased by the Devil."

"It wasn't the Devil, Eustice. It was the Sheriff. We were in the wrong place at the wrong time."

"What ever you say CP. But you say it was the police I say it was Satan, or at least one of his minions. Ain't make no difference. I gotta take you where I gotta take you. That's just the way it is."

"Where are we going Eustice?"

"A collsarn cornfield. I'm supposed to drop you off. You'll see, everything will be just fine. You're pal will be there. It's part of the grand design."

"Oh no, man. Grand design. You're going to take us to a cornfield--why?"

"I gotta drop you two off. I got work to do, I got orders to do this."

"Who tell you do dat?" Nell asked.

"They call him the doc. He's really some sorta wise fella been around a long time. He don't say it, but I know he's in cahoots with the good guys. He tells me he's from the future. Him and that gal he's always with, Milly, they say they's from 2070 and resettled in 1958 to keep the peace. I met `em when I took ill a few years back, and they call on me to run errands. I do odd jobs for `em but that's it. They ain't never said but for nothin' about their business. I just know what I know cause I know it."

"So you're an employee?" Nell said.

"Ma'am, I done died, went to the hereafter, and the doc's helped me out."

"Helped you out?" CP asked.

"Hellsfire. Folks thought I was plum looney, but Doc B showed `em all, he done showed me that there's holes in this corporeal life that go from one time to another.

"Why a cornfield?"

"It's the quickest way to get you to where you're supposed to be going," he said. "And go easy on the Early Times ma'am. I think I'm gonna need some spirits."

"Where are we supposed to be going?" CP asked.

"Yeah hillbilly boy, this place has a funky smell and I don't like it." Nell said.

"Yeah. There's something eerie about this place."

"Yep, it's a hole in the universe." Eustice said.

"What?"

"Smell that?"

"Yeah," It smelled like ozone, or that electrical sizzle that comes after the lightning bolt has struck.

"That means we're near the place that you ought be. Now go on, skedaddle." At that, the truck screeched to a halt. "Go on."

WHAT ALEJANDRO AND BART'S JOB REALLY WAS

"We gotta take thees thing and put eet in the place we're s'posed too, right?" Alejandro pointed his chin at the metronomic capitulator.

"No shit snapperbrain." Pinto jammed the car into park and said: "C'mon retard, let's get this over with."

"Okay, my focking shoulder hurts and I wanna get this over with."

"Moron, you DO know how to turn that thing on, right?"

"Yeah, iss simple. There's a switch that says on and off no beeg deal."

"Alright let's do it," Pinto said, unfastening his seat belt. Gimme that thing and we'll get this over with. I figure we'll put it about twenty or so feet away, and get our asses out of here."

"Ees a good plan, meng." Alejandro watched Bart Pinto take the device from the floorboard of the passenger seat where Alex was sitting, put it under his arm, and scan the field.

"There's nobody here but us, Alejandro, let's get this over with. C'mon."

The two men scoped out the area making sure no one followed them, and set the device down. Alejandro flipped the switch and the two errand boys high tailed it back to the car and waited.

"Meng, we been seetin' here forever and nothin's happenin' whass de story?"

"Shut the fuck up asshole. Something's gonna happen." Bart said as he rolled down his window.

The dense stalks of corn at midday blocked out the sun and waved in the wind as if they had lives of their own. He could swear the sound of the stalks sounded like whispering women telling secrets. Probably what a fuckup premature ejaculator Alejandro was.

A high pitched sound filled the car, the field, everywhere. It was so loud Pinto had to hit the brakes and cover his ears. Alejandro tried to scream about the sound but couldn't speak. And then there was contortion of the earth. A mirror like ripple appeared before them, and the world became a blur. Was it an earthquake, a tornado, some bizarre storm? They felt the car shake violently, and a pressure as if the atmosphere had changed suddenly. The car seemed to lift off the ground whipping them around harshly, forcefully, and the tug of their seat belts tightening made both men gasp as the car vanished from the field with an audible pop.

At that, Alejandro, Bart Pinto, and their car left the twenty-first century. In fact, they entered the eddies and flow in the space-time continuum. Neither of them had the presence of mind to wonder where it would take them.

Herman Duss looked on as the stage was set.

28

DROP OFF

Nearly one half mile away from the very place that Alejandro and Bart Pinto had left the twenty-first century CP and Nell stood facing each other, baffled. They were in the middle of a cornfield.

CP and Nell waved goodbye to the errand boy from time and space to walked into the cornfield.

"Nell did you get the license number of that truck?" CP said, staring at the stalks of corn. He squinted and looked at Nell. "I think there's a path . . . a road or something."

"CP, you know what we doin' here?" Nell said.

"No. But the hick sounded convincing, and something he said made sense."

"Yeah, like what?"

"Beaufort. I don't know if it was a dream, but I knew what he was talking about. The hick knew Grinder and said he'd be here."

"Where? We in the middle of a cornfield. That Grinder's a city boy, not some hick. How he find us?"

"The guy who dropped us off said so."

"You believe that cracker?"

"No, not really, but I believe this," CP held up a piece of paper. It was a map with an X in the center that said YOU ARE HERE, and a detailed pathway, using the sun, which was at it's zenith to navigate.

"I din't see him slip that to you." Nell stared at it for a few seconds, squinted, and saluted the sun, shielding her eyes. "Damn. That looks legit. When'd he slip dat to you?"

"When you were guzzling his booze," CP said.

"Dat true." Nell said. "I could use me some more dat."

"I think we ought to follow the trail."

"Yeah, I cool wit dat. Hey CP, whass all that shit about a time travel hole--a hole through time--a portal to 1958 to meet Doc Beaufort. What the fuck's that all about?"

"I guess we'll find out, Nell. Just keep walkin'"

"Damn mah feets hurt," she said.

"Take the fucking heels off, Nell."

"Dat a good idea. Okay I take off my top too?"

"Oh shit, man. I hope you have a bra on."

"You don't go lookin' my breastesses CP. You a doctor. And yeah, I got me a bra. You ain't gettin' no freebie."

CP and Nell brushed away shards of corn silt, and worked through the stalks like they were in a jungle. Finally they reached a clearing, and in it was a car, and a man standing next to it,

"Yo looky like we done found where we s'posed to be."

"I reckon so, Nell. I reckon so."

29

THE MEETING

GRINDER was leaning against his car a cigarette dangling from his lower lip, when this pickup truck pulls up with some redneck driving. CP and Nell the ho are in the cab. Shit. A fucking cornfield in the middle of nowhere. This'd better be good.

The car was parked exactly where the person on the phone said to. The latitude and longitude the man claimed, was where all things would come together and make sense. The "Or else," of the man's voice on the phone suggested an extra few slugs of booze. But the bits and pieces of knowledge the guy had sounded legit enough to bust a move.

It was high noon and the coordinates he'd put into his GPS led him right here. Smack dab in the middle of nowhere. He saw what must have been miles and miles of cornstalks and knew--as if from a dream-- that he'd been here before. In fact he was sure of it.

There were tire tracks in the soil. Not his--no. He knew his car's tracks. He started looking around--Was there a car, some other people? Eh, what the fuck? He heard some rustling among the stalks, and looked up to see his old pal, CP.

"CP, where the fuck've you been?" Grinder tossed his cigarette down and ground it out with the tip of his cowboy boot.

"Me? Where did you go? Better yet, how did you find me?"

"Buckaroo Bagwam had directions to where you were. It also had a phone number, Doc Beaufort's number. It was fucking long distance."

"Really, toll call?"

"Sixty fucking years SHIT. That'd be some serious bank CP. The phone number was to 1958, and he wants us to be there, said he'd guide us."

"I see both you boys ride off yesterday in Grinder's convertible. You was off to make some bank." Nell said.

"I don't remember," Grinder said. "How about you CP?"

"I woke up today in some friggin' mansion that went all funky like I was in a dream, passed out, and woke up in my usual digs. You?"

"I woke up in a friggin' old high class hotel that was empty. They were in the process of swingin' a wrecking ball."

"Bullshit," CP said.

"I kid you not, man. How the fuck do you know you weren't dreaming the whole thing?"

CP shrugged, "I don't."

"Where'd you boys go yessiday?" Nell said.

"I had a gig to go see patients out in the sticks, even have the address in my car," Grinder pointed his chin at the Cadillac parked among the stalks of corn.

"Whatever it was, I blacked out." CP said.

"I remember bein' here, man," Grinder said. "Then off to some bumfuck town."

"We're in the middle of a damned cornfield Grinder. Shit, my head hurts," CP rubbed his temple, and dug in his pocket.

"What're you doin' man?"

"Lookin' for a Percodan," CP said.

"You got another one?"

"Yeah, yeah," CP said producing a couple tablets and saying: "Why did we end up in a cornfield? Did we get that fucked up?"

"I got a phone call when I was at the bar," Grinder said. He was walking toward the Cadillac. "I'll get something to wash these down with."

Just as Grinder opened up the passenger door of the car, a loud growling sound filled the air. Grinder stopped in his tracks, looked over at CP and Nell. The three of them stood facing the same direction, the sound grew louder and the whump, whump, whump of a chopper rustled the tops of the corn stalks then flattened them out. One by one they looked up, then at each other.

A Vietnam War battle ready Huey hovered over them. They saw the chopper's armaments dangling beneath it like a boner on a Doberman, ready to let loose a spray of piss.

CP shoved Nell and Grinder toward a thick patch of stalks that hadn't been disturbed by the chopper blade's violent gusts. The three of them dove into the thicket and braced for the fall and safety among the roots and soil.

There was no floor, no base, no landing to roll on. They kept falling, as if caught in some swirling vortex, like a giant toilet's flush. They swirled free of the bounds of gravity. The sounds of the helicopter faded fast, and a high pitched syncopating rhythm seemed to pump them through the plumbing of some unseen space between spaces.

They bounced off the walls of an electrostatic cloud, like an electrically charged Polyester mattress. Crackling and buzzing as they fell toward some world other than the one they'd left.

30

WHEN DID YOU GET THAT CALL?

With an abrupt cessation of movement the three of them stared at each other, waited a few beats and took in their surroundings. The lay of the land, the sky, they sat there quietly for a a thick--what the fuck--moment. Finally CP said, "Shit. Where the hell are we?"

"More like when, good buddy, I think we're in 1958."

"How do you know that?"

"I got a call that said that I had to be here."

"So let's go see what the deal is." CP said, righting himself, and taking hold of Nell's arm.

"Hang on," Grinder said. "Let me scope it out first."

"Why?"

"I got the call from Herman Duss,"

"The chiropodist?"

"What did he want?"

"He said he shot a woman in the head in 1977."

"Holy shit. There's no statute of limitations on that."

"He called FROM 1977. He figured out how to use the portals."

"The fucking portals--Beaufort, the chips. Oh shit. I wasn't dreaming," CP said.

"Maybe you ought to lay off the pills, CP."

"Shut up, Grinder," CP said. "What's Duss up to?"

"He said that he was going to change history, and that proof of it was that he knew exactly where to find me. He said that he dropped a business card at the scene of the crime,"

"That was over forty years ago man." CP said.

"No. It was just now--today--for him it was 1977, and he left Beaufort's card"

"That means that if the cops go to Beaufort's office and shake him down in 1977 we'll be what?"

"I don't know." Grinder said, "But it can't be good."

"I called Beaufort. He said that I had to show up here, with you and Nell."

"What?"

"Look, over there, who dat man?"

From their vantage point in the alley, the three of them standing behind garbage cans, debris, a beat up car, and other junk they saw Herman Duss walking from his office. His path T-boned the alley. Seconds later a car pulled up and two men jumped out. CP and Nell recognized them immediately. They were from 2013 and tried to take Nell hostage.

31

TIME HAD STOOD STILL

Doc Beaufort's Office

On the outskirts of Big Town is a town lodged between Amish Country, farmland, and the quaint Shaker heritage the founders may have found suitable for settling a few hundred years ago. The fact that farming remained a staple for America's economy further enabled the small town's necessity.

The village of Hoogerstown may very well have looked as it had thirty, forty, or fifty years ago to someone passing through. The major thoroughfare, Main Street, was a Rockwellian depiction of the imagination of an American Dream someone could have, or should have ever had. It appeared to anyone visiting the rural districts of America's countryside as "cute, quaint, and wholesome." They couldn't have been more mistaken.

The town's politicos forbade the construction of chain stores, and made strict restrictions on the architecture and design of all new structures. Everything MUST remain compliant in order to build, operate, or function within this "Small Town USA," for which Hoogerstown had become known.

Life in Hoogerstown remained under the strict jurisdiction of the Town's mayor, it's city council, and governing bodies which permitted only those who met the standards set out in the 1950s to comply. For instance, a McDonald's Restaurant could indeed be built in Hoogerstown, but it's golden arches could not rise above the level of the treetops.

The buildings remained consistent with the design of the 1940s and 50s, and any "new" or "modern" construction was not permitted after the debacle of the previous decade. That's when the abominable monstrosity of a mall and adjoining office building erupted and disrupted the city's major unique quality. The Corman Corporation.

The Corman Corporation soon found the town's inhabitants--although seemingly underemployed--less than hospitable. And the "ultra-modern" complex was plagued with a series of disastrous events ultimately leading to the CC to relocate. The building remained uninhabited, as a reminder to any visitors to the town that there was no place for new development in Hoogerstown for outsiders. Nope. Not unless they were privy to the town's little secret. That all new construction be conducted underground.

Hoogerstown was built upon a rich labyrinth of cave laden bedrock, which sprawled for miles and miles beneath the village extending into the corn and wheat fields. A city beneath a city was one of America's best kept secrets for decades. In fact it wasn't until the year 2030 that the caves were put to use by one of the town's most influential, and enduring person: Doc Beaufort.

No one knew precisely how he came to such prominence, or particularly cared. His credentials were just fine, and his general medical practice served the town, the surrounding area, and the tiny hospital just fine.

Newcomers to Hoogerstown either took to the Doc, or they didn't. If they didn't they usually didn't spend more than a few hours, and a few dollars at the diner.

Time seemed to have worked differently in Hoogerstown. The long stemmed metal poles at every other block had huge white faced clocks, whose faces had Roman Numerals. Would seem to an outsider somewhat odd.

The absence of telephone or electric wires didn't come to mind until a passerby had been back on the interstate and miles away, and then it'd be too late to give much thought to.

The fact that there was no exit on the main highway for Hoogerstown made sense. After all, there wasn't much by way of amusement, entertainment, or sightseeing value. The truck stop and the train station were fifty miles on. Why would anyone visit this town that time, the highways, the world, pretty much left behind anyway?

Doc Beaufort's office was on the second floor of the five story medical building on Main Street. The elevator on the first floor had been broken for some time, and the staircase was right there in the lobby.

The entry was a glass door with a brass panel directory listing the names of the building's inhabitants, a dentist, chiropodist, lawyer, and an accountant. There may have been some uninhabited offices, but that was just fine for the building's owner of record, Doc Beaufort.

The building's original owners dated back nearly a century and could be viewed at the town's clerk of courts office across the street next to the sheriff's office.

Flanking the entryway of Doc Beaufort's building was a pharmacy on one side, a furniture store on the other. An office supply company that hadn't been bought out by one of the big chains, and as a nod and a wink courtesy, it remained in business, despite steep prices. Was it because the town's people did not want "outsiders" coming to Hoogerstown? Maybe..

Things were according to the townspeople, just swell. And so they were, until the rumbling red `58 Cadillac

Convertible pulled up along the curb of the medical building. A man, with a leather jacket got out, failed to put change in the parking meter, flicked his cigarette onto the pavement, and combed his hair staring at his reflection in the glass door.

He gave himself a nod of approval, removed the pack of smokes for another, and took a swig from the pint of liquor he'd taken from the glove box of his vintage car.

32

Doc B

Atop the last step to the second floor was a wooden door lit by a flickering neon light, and on the metal elevator door a paper with the words "out of order" neatly printed on it. Five steps past it is a carpeted hallway, with a window at either end illuminated by natural light. You're immediately greeted by the cloyingly sweet smells from the dentist's office to the left, and the sound of gentle whirring of a dental drill. To the right the first door had the name Dr. Beaufort, General Practice engraved in a metal plaque.

Opening the door set off a soft ding-dong, doorbell sound, immediately you felt a shift in the atmosphere. The temperature was a few degrees cooler although there was no air conditioning, and your ears popped, as if you were on an airplane about to level off at flying altitude. You couldn't put your finger on exactly what the sensation was, and probably wouldn't, because you'd be struck by the meticulously ornate waiting room. The comfortable looking dark leather sofas with creases and brass buttons were inviting. They faced each other across the burled wood magazine table, with little lion's heads at their base. Even the matching wooden chairs lined up, looked cozy. They had the name of some university scrawled on them, and the end tables with ornate brass lamps and shades glowed warmly. Just being there made you feel a notch better than you did before you set foot in the office. There were paintings on the dark green walls of countrysides, and fox hunts, and little lights illuminating them. The ancient National Geographic, Time, and Life magazines seemed to be placed just so, to remind you that this was a doctor's office. The pebble glass window next to an inner door confirmed it.

Behind the sliding glass was a woman in a peaked nurse's cap, and half-moon shaped glasses resting at the end of a small nose. She wore no makeup, and could have been in her twenties or forties. Like the office itself emitted a comforting field an aura of sorts, that generated a warmth that seemed--to those unaccustomed to the concept--genuinely concerned and caring.

The first time visitor might notice that there was no computer, or any electronic devices at all. How could something be so all wrong about something that was so all right? A conundrum to some, but not to today's visitor. He knew where he was, and why he was there.

"Milly," the man said as he rapped on the pebble glass window. "Open up woman, I know you're hidin' in there."

The man standing in front of the window had a cigarette dangling from his lower lip, and tapped his left foot while he fished around his pocket searching for his lighter. Finally fishing it out, rolling his thumb on the mechanism two, three, four, "What the fu . . . ?" Milly reached her her hand out so fast, the leather jacketed man couldn't dodge it. She took the tobacco stick with one hand of long delicate fingers from his mouth, and broke it in half.

"Grinder?" She said the faintest of surprise in her tone.

"No, I'm the friggin' Pope?"

"I thought you were . . . relocated?"

"Do I look relocated, Milly? I gotta see Beauf. Is he here?"

"He's with patients," Milly was standing up leaning on her fingertips, staring at this throwback Elvis sideburned, middle-aged man, reeking of booze. "You drove here?"

"No, I friggin' flew here."

"Grinder you were declared dead."

"Do I look dead to you sweetie?"

"This isn't going to go well," she said raking a hand across the side of her head tucking in a few stray straw-blonde strands behind her ear, and shaking her head. "Where's CP?"

"I thought you'd know?"

At that moment a man's voice said: "Well well well, look what the Schrödinger's Cat dragged in."

"Doc," Grinder said. "How's it goin' man?"

"I think we need to chat Grinder, " he said. "Buzz him in."

33

Doc Beaufort sizes up Grinder

"Well well well, Neal Grinder, forgive me if I'm not at all surprised to see you."

"Fuck you man. Do you know what happened?"

"Calm down, son."

"I ain't doin' shit," Grinder put a tobacco stick in his mouth, grabbed the nearest chair and sat backwards on it. "What the fuck is going on?"

"Milly," Beaufort whispered into the intercom on his desk. "Get him some coffee."

"Listen Beaufort we's going to discuss this experience with time travel. Isn't that special?

"Please be patient Grinder, you have a propensity to embellish things."

"Embellish my ass." Grinder said, lighting up.

"By the way Beaufort, I got CP and Nell with me. They're downstairs. Don't worry they ain't gonna touch anything or talk to anyone. We know we're here for a reason, and they sent me up here to see if you'll come clean, you know fess up on what's going on. None of us, me, Nell, CP, or that chick CP thought he was with yesterday makes any sense. But I got a call that said I was supposed to be HERE. Some asshole said he was going to change history. He said that he was gonna make sure some of the shit that's supposed to happen ain't gonna happen the way it's supposed to, and he figured out how to rig things so he'd be the friggin' boss of the planet. Tell me, was the motherfucker full of shit, or what?"

Beaufort stood up, walked to the door, and left Grinder alone with the pot of coffee, and cup.

34

BEAUFORT REALIZES THERE IS A FUTURE IN CHANGING THE PAST AND IT'S NOT GOOD

"Milly, there's something off-kilter with the satellites and supercomputers governing us." The reality he and Milly have been guardians was awry.

The chiropodist across the hall wasn't supposed to have died, disappeared, or done anything but get old. Instead according to Beaufort's records--a holographic history book--not really a book at all but a book of history that hasn't yet happened. More of a Rand McNally of who things are supposed to be.

"He was here less than an hour ago, tossed the computer at me, and already there are some ripples in the space-time continuum,"

Beaufort peeks into Herman Duss's office, and instead of finding the kindly middle aged chiropodist he finds another man--Luke Ponzetti, another chiropodist. He introduces himself, and realizes that Duss's natural successor was a man of African descent. Who was supposed to be there, isn't. Duss must have found a portal, stepped through it, and fucked up history.

He returns to his Holohistory Guide. Duss DID find a portal and end up in the future, and the past! He'd taken the molybdenum based substance, the son-of-a-bitch. Beaufort had to double check the office supplies. It was missing, the material necessary to make the Mymine DNA chip laced substance, that he kept in vials, and the crystalline fluid that resonated the time portals. Shit it was gone. That alone was imperative for time travel.

"I knew he was up to something when he tossed the computer at me. Duss must have swiped them. Damn it. He was infused, and accessed the time charts," Beaufort was flummoxed. "He used what he'd taken to make something other than its purpose, he must have taken something from his old office too. It could have been anything, but Duss traveled to the year 1976 and future history books reflect that he extended the field of chiropody out of his own greed. Making devices people wore in their shoes, and made a lethal tracking pair for Nadine's great grandmother, assuring she'd not be born. The prick killed her, and must have taken the mymine laced inserts. Son of a bitch. Beaufort scanned his own body, the implanted DNA was beginning to decay, He ran through a series of tests on himself. Discovering after a series of calculations time, for him, Milly, and the future he'd come from was deteriorating. Duss, that prick had set off a time paradox that would jeopardize history's linear flow.

He had to find him, bring him back here and ablate that portion of his mind that recalled any of it. But no that wouldn't be necessary. He had to find where Duss went first.

Which portal, where and when did he leap, and what change did he first attempt before murdering the founder of the chip, Nadine's father.

He was still alive, the time paradox hadn't rippled immediately as the theorists predicted. It would take at least twenty-four earth hours until the impact came. A wave-a tsunami of sorts, but it would come, and when it did Beaufort, and the future he came from would cease to exist. Fucking space-time continuum.

"Milly," he called out from his study. "Have Grinder get his friends from the car, unlock the doors to the caves, and get them down there. We're going to 1936!"

35

DICEY 1958
The Long Aftermath of the Alleged American Dream

It never was any dream . . . just another binge. The country was drunk on prosperity before ringing up the bills that'd never get paid. Before the next major war showed up to wipe out the competition.

Doc Beaufort sat at his desk in what would some day be called any town USA, and stared out the window. It would have that nuanced feel of what nostalgics referred to as a "simpler time" in American modern history.

It was Hoogerstown, another one of many of America's Hometown communities equipped with that sense for another few decades. Its architecture was marked by well constructed buildings with running water, flushing toilets, showers and baths shipped from bustling factories no longer manufacturing ordinance, machine guns, rifles, pistols or bombs.

The carpentry was precise as the makeshift forts and headquarters scattered across the battlefields. As were all the electrical systems. Precisely wired as they were on the bombers and machines of war by men who built them as if lives depended upon them. Things were put together by men who took more than pride in their work, they built things that stayed built as if lives, which they very well did, depended upon precision.

Doc Beaufort marveled at the telephone poles with little metal rungs for men to climb in case there was some power issue on the lines that supplied electricity and telephone services. The sidewalks cleaner than the barracks latrines on any military base, and the crisp neat clothing worn by men and women alike manufactured by pleasantly employed Americans who once made uniforms for millions. Now they had safe secure jobs in factories and plants that made everything once designed for a war effort, this side, the Americans had won.

All the resources of this huge nation and its populace vectored in on making things better so no soldier would be left on a battlefield or in a war zone in the air, sea or land with shoddy equipment.

Automobiles with huge engines manufactured in plants that built tanks, Half-tracks which competed with Schützenpanzerwagens a few years back. The steel mills still buzzed to make new pleasure ships instead of warships, made the thick steel doors of the cars that rumbled down newly paved streets by former Army Corps of Engineers who'd found fine occupations constructing highways of the meticulous industrialism stemming from men who'd survived having stormed the beaches Normandy, the battles across Europe, or those in the Pacific. He was pleasantly comfortable with the world as it happened to be at this particular time in human history.

Beaufort knew it would take a while for America to wake up from the so-called American Dream. Especially since it was more of a binge drunk than a dream, and hangovers didn't really have any waking up from, they just had to run their course.

It was WWII that planted the seeds of prosperity in the mind's of its survivors. America's factories which were haunts for hobos, farmland that'd become dustbowl hectares, and homelessness was the rule rather than an exception.

America was in a pickle and the only way to bring prosperity to the States was to wipe out the competition. Once the Sudetenland ceded and the blitzkrieg raged, Germany began to re-arm in the 30s. Japan too, steel mills, automobiles, electrical gizmos, and of course weapons. Busy busy bad guys--so they were--readied their elaborate armies for war.

No country in any other epoch has enjoyed so much prosperity, so little crime, and it's people so enthusiastic about a future with so much on the horizon. World War II ended thirteen years ago essentially wiping out all the competition.

Beaufort looked out the window. 1958, the pinnacle of America's global dominance.

He stared at the traffic light that signaled a time to stop that mammoth growling beast of a Chevrolet, Olds or Cadillac with the tail fins of a fighter plane or the larger rumbling trucks packed with fresh food and goods. Click green and traffic ran smoothly through an intersection, pedestrians neatly dressed, women pushing baby carriages, and nicely frocked well mannered children obeying the machines telling them "Don't Walk" and waiting when the traffic signal clicked to yellow, then stopping as did the cars at red.

Everything was so simple, and precise. The collective worries were about an invisible enemy who might explode an Atomic Bomb. The lethal destroyer of cities, that no one would dare use because all the niceness of the world wasn't limited to Any Town USA, but in varying degrees across the globe where similar towns sprang up with small variations.

This is why Doc Beaufort left his home in 2070 to relocate in a time before the machines became the masters. And the stoplight wasn't just going click click click, it was dictating the lives of every living human on the planet. Soon all the planets that had colonies populated by humans.

Ah but no more for Beaufort. He'd come to 1958 a few years ago with his female, Milly on what would be called a vacation. People traveled through time in his era. They could have gone to Ancient Rome, the Roaring Twenties, Pre-Civil War America, you name it, you could go anywhere anytime for the right price. Time travel in 2070 was to the semi-affluent what air travel was to the world of late twentieth century. Foolproof, simple, painless, and hardly as awkward as it was when the portals were first discovered ten years earlier.

The portals were found by accident as doors of sorts that opened up into what some theorists called inter-dimensional transference stations. They were indeed areas where the laws, if there really were any, solid precepts in the space-time continuum.

The first portal was found by Emmet Seeney on his farm outside of Des Moines, Iowa in 2058. He was inspecting the irrigation system when a thunderstorm obviated the need to waste precious water. He'd taken his hover car out into the field when a lightning bolt catapulted across the sky, and as he later described seemed to linger between the clouds and then suddenly redirected toward his hover car, struck it, and set off its alarm system that made a beep beep beep sound in the key of G minor the former key used in India. Prior to that all cars honked in the key of F.

In combination with the bleeps in G minor of his Mumbai made hover car, the lightning and crackling wisps of the stalks of corn a certain geophysical phenomenon occurred that brought time, space, and what some physicists speculated a wormhole type gap in the landscape that landed on the other side of something.

What that something was had been anyone's guess. Until some hapless happy go lucky wage earner decided to stick his head into the portal. It was called a portal because what had been created remained open, a gash in the fabric of time, space, geography, topography, and unlike anything before seen by humans-or at least spoken or written of. It, the shimmering mirror like wall, the size of a garage door for a 1990s era SUV-couldn't be moved, shaken, or disturbed. It seemed to just appear, after thousands of variations of car horns, rustling crops, and lightning jolts under certain circumstances. It had the depth of a mirror, in other words, it had no depth, only some dimensionality indescribable. But there it was, the shimmery thing in the cornfield. It could be summoned, but it wasn't until Clay Doomis, an employee of Emmet Seeney stuck his drunken head into it, yanked it out with an audible pop, and told Yetty May, his sometime girlfriend, and full time beautician who only had sex for money with fellas she knew, that he saw a whole different world, egads in the middle of Mr. Seeney's cornfield!

And thus began the mass exodus to this quaint little part of the world to see this mysterious gap in the fabric of reality and the beginnings of a new age. The same triad of phenomenon sprang up around the globe and portals such as this were found all over. Some grand entrepreneur and crew set out to open the first wholesale gallery of history, which grew into strolls in the past, and finally there were well equipped explorers who visited these pasts discovering that human beings in the 2060s could travel back in time but that there was a catch: you could not change history, you could not interfere with the past, you would gradually forget what you thought you knew about the future the harder you tried to remember a future that hasn't happened yet. Hmm that was perplexing and bad guys tried to figure out a way to scam around this so they could make some bank on stock picks, sporting events, patents, and so on.

But nothing seemed to work. The human mind was incapable of retaining information that wasn't in it. Nope, many tried taking recording devices but they were rendered useless because they weren't in existence before a jaunt into the past.

And then the mix of medicine and time travel was born.

At about the same time these portals were discovered the earth was plagued with electromagnetic radiation induced cancers. The discovery of specific means to fight cancer on a genetic basis evolved by way of the vanities of women trying to look younger than they were. They wanted to fill the gaps wrinkles created, and the DNA needed to generate new proteins that'd become the intracellular matrices of connective tissue.

It worked so well that the electronically guided proteins were able to be directed to sagging jowls, boobs, and chicken's feet. The über proteins could also make their way to diseased flesh, wipe out cancers, and activate parts of the brain most humans didn't know existed. For the first time in history human's could read each others minds. And that was no great treat. Many went insane, but we'll get back to that later.

The major side effect of this new protein redirection was that some people could be implanted with a nanotechnologically constructed submolecular cyclic nucleotide that could be implanted in humans-for a hefty fee-and they'd never age, never get sick, and be able to read minds. And if they wished to travel through time, retain what they knew. The past was fertile ground for social engineering and the mistakes of the past could, with some discretion be corrected, modified or flat out changed to serve some political whim of whoever was in charge. Politics in the year 2070 took on a whole new meaning because a President or Czar, King or Queen could be elected to their position from thousands of years in the past.

What a world it was, Doc Beaufort thought to himself as he sat there with his feet on his desk staring out at the stoplight in 1958. He was one such sentinel from 2070, whose duty was to make sure no scoundrels, thieves, history revisionists, or other such miscreants made their way into his epoch to screw things up for the future. That willingness to settle centuries before his natural time, was his prize, his compensation for being part of a loosely knit group of guardians. They were Historical Stability Regulators, and it was a job of joy for people longing for simpler lives not governed by the machines. Having his woman companion, Milly with him made for a pretty decent life as a country doctor who could cure any disease with future technology, sniff out the thoughts of bad guys, and stamp out crooked crap before it had a chance to happen. He dug his job very much, until he didn't. That was when the unexpected just showed up at his door.

Who what why and how were the first questions he asked . . .

"Milly," he called out. "Have the people with Grinder wait for me at the elevator. I have to see about our neighbor."

"Duss?" She said.

"Yes, I believe that Dr. Duss found a portal, and traveled through time without being readied, and tampered."

36

Beaufort Gathers Himself And Explains The Need to Regroup

As soon as we realized that the chiropodist Duss had made off with several vials of the quantum resonance (QR) fluid, mymine laced platelet rich plasma in pre-filled syringes, we knew something had to be done, fast.

Thankfully Duss hadn't caused any immediate paradox, and even if he had we were well stocked. Nonetheless time was wasting. Duss certainly could have gleaned some of the data from his toying in my study. Especially with enhanced mental agility. Yes, he would know the extent of the QR substance, the crystalline substance, the miscible admixture of material consisting of molybdenum, nanoparticles, and subatomic resonators. He's surely opening portals. The rascal left the charts askew, as if I wouldn't notice. Perhaps the freshly brilliant WANTED me to see what he knew, the fool. He knows that he can disrupt the resonating atoms anywhere, anytime, and find the portals of his choosing. Some of the vials Duss had taken were aerosol sprays. Simply point, press, and a portal opens, and the fluid, all that's needed is to dab it on a surface and it becomes subject to opening a chasm in the space-time continuum.

First things first: Get back to 2070, hopefully things hadn't changed, at least not yet. And find the last few people who'd been resettled, if they were there, and then regroup. Find Duss and place him at his office where nature will have to take its course.

We, Milly and I, went to the laboratory beneath the building, and studied the time logs. Charts that are expressed visually by delightful computer generated images of historical events, Let me digress for a moment. The time logs scenarios (TLS) look like this: Picture a very large pool table with little towns and villages, like an elaborate model railroad train mock up, only this is the world, so it's a very big mock up. Now with a few clicks, words, or phrases, different parts of life on earth can appear. For instance I can say: Ancient Rome, mention the city, the people, or a specific person, and the combination of laser and holographic images will appear. Simultaneously the same surface can appear above that plane on the pool table. Like the pages of a book one over the other I can generate what is happening at one point in history at a specific geographical locale, and many many others layered on top, or to the sides of the period being studied. So if I were to move around a piece on the field--a ball on the pool table, so to speak--I can see how those ramifications affect events in different times, places, and if I want narrow it down to individual people. Yes, technology has gotten that detailed. In fact I can know what a person from 1928 was going to be doing in five, ten, or even twenty years simply by summoning the proper time logs and layering them on top of each other. This became more detailed with the advent of the internet and the tracking and tracing in many ways got simpler.

Needless to tell you that it is a very large laboratory and sometimes a visitor will show up from 2070 or beyond to update our TL generated from the supercomputing devices. The fellow Lorenz, and his "Butterfly Effect" is truly reflective of what our time log scenarios is capable of. In fact the notion that someone can change history, although in some cases noble, more often it's not.

Greed abounds in the human, and it's our job:mine, Milly, some folks from the Time Bureau, to insure that the book the big book, on how things--history that is-- must remain intact so as not to disrupt the outcome of the future. If it does we wouldn't be here.

The supercomputers have this factored in. If there is going to be a variation say someone tries changing something in the past that might alter the future, the self-preserving --some would say self-serving-- supercomputers and the activity would be "naturally" curtailed. Hmm. Let me try to clarify why the silly notion that you can go back in time and change the future is not possible, and that what we do is a fail safe of sorts. Oh there have been many many people who thought they could get away with timecropping, that's what we call it when someone decides they want to stake out a place in human history using their knowledge of future events. As we've mentioned, in order to move about through different times or eras, your body has to be adjusted to withstand the forces the physical universe places upon our molecular, atomic structures.

The additional nucleotide was one, but there's a bit more, and that's usually what prevents people from screwing up the past. It's an odd physical phenomenon like upon awakening from a dream you forget what you've dreamt. Early time travelers, those who chanced upon the portals, found that once they entered a place in the past, they couldn't recall what happened in the future because, for them, it hasn't occurred yet. This was just fine, but more sophisticated time cheats made all sorts of cues, clues, hints, and reminders were clear violations of the space-time continuum bylaws. But it was done all the time, and they've found that some odd quirk of the physical universe kicks in and forces their bodies to malfunction.

For instance telling someone who'd win the World Series in 1939 may be something you know, but you'd be physically unable to do anything about it. Because for each epoch there is a universal harmonic, a tune for every time. You'd naturally fumble because the subsonic tones would befuddle the unprepared time traveler. For every moment of existence there exists a a harmonic; which has been categorized, registered, logged, and calculated within nanoseconds of any cellular reaction. Things that you think can happen have no bearing on things that simply can't happen. Maybe at some point before the computers began to build upon themselves someone could sneak through a portal and try to do something. But they died. Their bodies cellular processes, chemical reactions fail because they would not be in tune with the era.

Oddly the old time astrologers may have been on to something, but they couldn't put the pieces together because they lacked the technology. The machines calculations are so extensive they can take the tone, the harmonics ,based upon the gravitational pull of the sun, the earth's axis, the pull of the moon, many many things working in confluence. Specific to one time and one time only, moments occurring once and only once under specific gravitational, solar, galactic movement. Remember the earth is part of a solar system that's part of a galaxy that's moving through the universe. The computers have factored those things in, so that an event on earth (or anywhere else really) can only happen once and that's it. A change to that event is measurable and adjusted, so as not to jeopardize future events.

Calculations going out infinitely, constantly clicking and ticking until they--the supercomputers--can calculate how many raindrops would need to hit the ground until the image of the Mona LIsa could be formed. Forgive me if I'm getting ahead of myself.

Now there are variations and sometimes they can cause some harm to future events. There are anomalies in the space-time continuum, as there are in all of nature.

Even though randomness is factored in, the nature of human beings is to a degree not within the broad range of predictability. Simply if someone truly wanted to screw up history and damage the future they can-to an extent. Although minimal it throws the harmony of the universe out of line, and can be cataclysmic. So the flapping of a butterfly's wings in Burma can indeed cause directly, and the computers show it, and I can watch it in my laboratory on the TLS, the time log scenarios.

Now now now, you probably are asking how some folks go sightseeing in time, right? As mentioned bodies can be modified genetically. They had to be because the darn portals kept springing up, some cosmic shift on the earth's axis back in 2030 or so. People'd just be minding their own business and fall into another dimension,or period in time. But by then computers were already self-replicating, the math was becoming more and more calculable. We had to adapt, and did so just fine to accommodate.

We made DNA mutation just a regular part of life, and that made time hopping just like what they'd call in America "as easy as pie." But if and only IF you're body had been prepared via an oscillating quantum tensegrity of the bioelectric field surrounding your body at any given time. Your cells had to be prepared hence, the mymine chip that modified the DNA. That also made your cells more malleable to be retuned just like holding up a tuning fork to tune a piano. In fact Milly and I have a Quantum Tensegrity Oscillator in the doorway of our office, so people can come and go and exchange ideas without being shut down.

So here we are in this vexing situation where someone swiped some mymine, and miscible fluid, and oscillatory fluid, that can open a portal anywhere, anytime, and with the right calculations pretty much predict when and where it leads.

Yesterday's visitors arrived--they were expected nonetheless. Yes, that would have been the two young men from 2012, and Nadine, one of my trainees from 2070.

I had to locate them all, and bring them here. The men may not have complete recollections of yesterday, and their genetic alterations. But CP and Grinder, a pair of young MDs who had no history in their times, they were sent to 2070 to balance off the universe.

That was that. They were neatly in the place where they should be, and the cosmos was in balance. My job, to usher them into harmony with the universe was done. And now this nonsense?

Herman Duss, the chiropodist who should have died in 1958 is back. The TLS reads that he's going to tamper with history? No no no, he's gone off to play games with the cosmic lottery.

Well,so far and we can't predict how long it will last he's created a time wave, and according to the time log scenarios is beginning to make the orchestrations of history somewhat off-kilter.

37

Beaufort, Milly, CP, Grinder and Nell have to go back to get back where the belong . . .

CP, GRINDER, NELL, BEAUFORT AND MILLY ARE AT BEAUFORT'S OFFICE

"Come along folks." Beaufort leads them to his laboratory deep in the earth. "The elevator's never been out of order.

The ride on what twenty years from then would have been an aging Otis, but in 1958 was sort of newish struck the passengers as a smooth riding gondola. It was more than just an elevator car, it was a Jules Verne Nautilus styled cab with ornate railings made from the finest woods, and dark green walls that had sconces to light it up, casting a nineteenth century style country gentleman's study look. Beaufort's idea of what an elevator should look like, especially one that was taking its passengers to his lair.

No one was quite sure how long the ride lasted, but long enough to tickle Grinder's urge for a smoke, make Nell ask when she could pee, and CP wonder out loud if the gondola had a mini-bar. To which, Beaufort replied: "Chop chop Milly. Make a note of that. Install bar ASAP," and just as he finished the phrase there was a thump. Just like that the cab came to a halt.

"My friggin ears are poppin'," Grinder rubbed the sides of his head. "How far down are we?"

"Beneath the deepest missile silos. We wouldn't want to disturb those folks now would we? Now please, let's step into my laboratory." He gestured them out, stating, "Milly, Nell, please, lady's first."

"It's chilly down here," CP cupped his hands and blew into his palms, looked up and down at the stalactites and stalagmites. "How did this get built, this shaft, the hydraulics, all of it?"

"This was an early silo site that was abandoned because of the network of caves. They were deemed unsuitable because of the radiation levels. Radon. My associates from 2070 arranged to be transported here made sure of it."

"Like they made sure of that friggin' thing?" Grinder was pointing at golf-cart type vehicle that seated six, maybe eight.

"Yes," Beaufort said. "Yes indeed. Now please join me and we'll take a short ride, and get ourselves ready."

"I gots to pee," Nell said.

"Now, now, Nell. We'll be at the lab soon."

Once aboard the shuttle Milly took the wheel, and they sped off with a launch whiplashing the passengers down a dark trail that looked to Grinder as if Knight's Templar built it.

"They did Grinder," Beaufort said.

"That's right you can read friggin' minds. What the fuck were they doing here?"

"Pretty much what we are. Traveling through time, experimenting with what they discovered beneath the ruins. Read your history books later. For now just consider that they were lost, and used this as a shelter, infirmary, and hideout from the indigenous people above."

Grinder socked that information away. Someday he'd find a way back here to score.

"Don't even think about it Grinder," Milly chimed in. "The location is impossible to find."

"Zat so?" Nell was staring at the vaulted natural geology, the jagged rocks, and eerie lighting that came from glowing lamps along the way. "Who puts in dem lights?" She stared at the vaulted ceilings, buttressed cross bars of concrete and metal beams.

"Oh folks have been coming here for centuries," Beaufort said. "This is sort of a headquarters, a jumping off point for time travelers. A way station if you will, so many many people with many many years of experience built this up to a standard that would meet anyone's expectations."

"Anyone who chose to take a trip through time." Milly added.

"Yes. That's correct, this is." Beaufort, seated next to Milly put his arm over the seat and turned to face CP, Nell, and Grinder. "Folks in the future had little choice in terms of vacationing, and interplanetary travel was more of a roughneck sort of thing. But finding a place in time to spend a holiday? Ah, it couldn't be beaten. Oh it did cost a bit, but no more relatively speaking than a time-share, or condo in South Beach. And for those who wanted to relocate for extended stays, or to do work for the Time Relocation Services, the TRS, like Milly and I, and of course Nadine, this was ideal as a jumping off point.

A few minutes later they emerged from the tunnel into an immense area with hundreds of doors, openings to tunnels, electronic equipment, and walls and walls several stories high of books. There were charts, pictures, and maps all over the domed room that was the size of two football fields.

"This is the Grand Central of Time Travel," Beaufort said.

"Well, where be the bat room?" Nell said.

"Let me drop you off. When you're finished, make a right, another right, and come in."

"Say what? What's 'in' supposed to mean?"

"He means the office," Milly added.

Beaufort's Underground Office.

"How come the place is empty?" Grinder said, lighting up a cigarette.

"It isn't," Beaufort snatched it out of his mouth. "There are hundreds of people coming and going whom you cannot see because they're doing so at different times. They're here, and they're not here."

"So what's with this place, where do all the doors lead?"

"Well, well, well, finally the right question."

"Okay what's the right answer?"

Beaufort sat down behind a desk whose top could have been made of quartz, or some other crystal. There were crystals, and glass like tubes, chalices, and devices all over.

"All of those doors lead to portals that lead to particular points in time and space. They're very specific, and unchangeable. Some go directly to . . . say, a speakeasy in the roaring 20s. Another to Ancient Rome, and some my my there's no telling. Folks enter and never return. They're all brought together in this hub," he spread his arms, "and you can choose where you would like to go. Some of course are forbidden as they lead to battlefields, crime scenes, horrible places. Whereas others are long journeys through the tunnels to some of the earth's most delightful locales. All for a life to be lived." He smiled, and the light caught his front teeth in just such a way that added a glimmer of sparkle that CP would later recall had to have been staged.

CP added: "For a fee, right?"

"You betcha," Beaufort closed his mouth.

"However, there's been some issues, and that's . . . "

"That's why you brought us here, right? Us stragglers, two out of work docs, a ho, and you need us to make something right that went wrong. Go on, I know the gig, this time travel schtick is for the well heeled, they're in every epoch. Yeah, E fucking pock. Don't look at me like some kinda crumb."

"You is a crumb," Nell said. Walking in fixing her miniskirt."

"You're right Grinder. You and CP wouldn't be able to pay for a time hop, but you fell into one and it created a paradox. From there adjustments were made by the orbiting satellites, and things would have been fine. You jumped through an uncharted portal,"

"Wha he talkin' `bout? Look at all this high falutin science shit, and he tell you they ain't got it all figgered out? That bullshit. I think you bein' set up for some fuck up from future man and his skinny ass white girl. Thass what I think. I think he need our asses to get hisself outta some big jam, right?"

"Yeah Beaufort, is she right?" CP, who'd been standing with his arms folded across his chest, leaning against the wall took a step forward. "Is she," he planted a fist on the crystal desk top.

Beaufort looked at Milly who was standing beside him. They locked eyes, and if they room could have gone quieter all those miles beneath the earth's surface it would have.

The scratch and snap of Grinder flicking a kitchen match with his thumbnail broke the silence. He took a drag from his cigarette, and blew out the smoke. "You need us don't you?"

"What's in it for us?" CP walked toward Beaufort, put his palms on the desk, and stared at Beaufort. "What?"

"You might just get to be born. If you're lucky. If you're real lucky that dream you had of waking up next to a beautiful woman in a mansion by the sea might come true. And Nell, you might get out of that racket and have a life."

"Whass wrong wit my life honkey?"

"Yeah, what?" Grinder said, looking at Nell as if for the first time. Not bad, he thought to himself. He could clean this ho up real nice. Yeah.

"Stop thinking Grinder." Milly said.

Beaufort spoke in in an icy tone: "I can't say much, but anything beyond doing tricks for peanuts in the crappiest part of the crappiest city in America in 2013 has to be more cheerful, and add years to your pre-destined time of death. Which according to history was written,. logged, and stored before you were born, not long from what it had been."

"I make my own destiny, gramps. So spare me the sweetheart speech. I just want to get the fuck out of here."

"Okay." Beaufort said. "I think that puts us on the same page."

"What we gotta do?

"Find a chiropodist." Milly said.

"Say what? I ain't gots not foots prollems."

"Not just any chiropodist. A man who used to have an office across the hall from me. A man whom would have lived out his natural life if it wasn't for Grinder, CP, and Nadine who he followed into a portal. Herman Duss, and his 1958 mind learned more about time travel and technology than anyone of his era, and used it. His greed grew, and he decided that being a chiropodist wasn't just punishment, he wanted to destroy the world as it was, and create his own. He wants Germany to win the war, and slavery be resurrected."

"You said 'wants' not the past tense," CP said.

"That's correct. Duss is in the act of changing history as we speak, and I need you three to stop him."

"Why us?"

"Your lives are intertwined. When you two, CP and Grinder, fell into the portal from 2012 to 1958 you met Nadine who was from 2070. The Sheriff was on to you, he was with the Time Enforcement Bureau. They keep people from dispelling or changing events. But he was as we suspected as corrupt as could be, and your presence in 1958 was expected, and to be used to smoke out the Sheriff. Which worked and if things went according to plan--history as it was written--you would have returned to your lives, and that would be that. But it didn't, you fell for Nadine, and vice versa CP. Her destiny was to return to 2070, and she did with you. That house on the beach was real, and Nell was perfectly content in that time, living a productive life as a time travel guide. But Grinder told Duss how to make money as a chiropodist, a procedure on feet that Duss used when he followed you into the 1970s. He became . . . "

"What the fuck's that shit: he became?"

"He became 'The Cobbler' and discovered the portal system. And began leaping through them, one after the other. Getting wealthier, evading other Time Enforcement agents, and finally decided that he wanted to--Beaufort shook his head--do what all humans do when they get a little power, he wanted it all. He wanted to rule the world."

"Shit," CP said.

"Yes. It can be real shitty," Milly added. "If we don't stop him the first few waves of time paradoxes will begin. And gradually what we know, what we--Beaufort and I--maintain . . . "

"Homeostasis or balance of the universe, at least earth's, will be tossed horribly off-kilter." Beaufort shook his head and stared at the tops of his hands.

"So you're sayin' that we gotta find this fucker, and nab him before he fucks up history."

"Yes."

"How're we gonna do that?"

"Not let him come in contact with Jesse Owens in 1936, and not shoot Nadine's great grandmother in 1977," Beaufort said matter-of-factly. "Are you up for it?"

"I still wanna know what's in it for me," Grinder said.

"That drunk in the bar, Poop?"

"Yeah, I remember that guy, a real jerkoff. What about him?" He was going to kill you that day. Shoot you dead in the parking lot."

"Okay then. I guess you can deal me in."

"Milly, let's get ready for a little trip."

38

1936

Beaufort, CP, Grinder, Milly, and Nell changed clothes, and were nearly finished dressing up in their period era threads when Beaufort said: "This is going to happen very quickly, so be prepared to do nothing."

"I can do that," Grinder said. "This cloth itches," he was scratching himself.

"Where did you get this shit Doc, central casting?"

"Something like that," Beaufort led them toward the sliding door of the elevator in the building's basement.

We're going to be walking into another era, so be careful what you do or say to anyone. Don't speak.

"I don't talk German, so no sweat," Grinder said.

"I know how to say you wants a blow job in twelve languages," Nell said, but not in German.

"Nell. I don't think that will be necessary." Beaufort shook his head.

"Let's go. This is going to happen fast. I have his coordinates."

Each of the portals had one destination, a confluence of time where the crack in its fabric began. That doorway to space-time continuum led to the year 1936, and to a location where that break in time's linear direction occurred. The Olympic Village in 1936, specifically the American Sector, the dormitories where the contestants lived.

"Man CP, you look like a real badass Nazi. Cool friggin' medals. The boots match that holster, yeah. Zere a gun in there? A luger, man those are friggin' cool. You know what those sell for at gun shows?"

"Shut up grinder." Beaufort said.

"Man look at you, Doc. That is some friggin' getup, the peaked hat, the braids, the Iron Cross. Shit, man, you look like the Red Barron. Like some high-fucking-ranking-officer in that black on black get up. What rank am I supposed to be? You must be a general, right?"

"Well well well, I am a Herr General boys. General Beaufort, ha. You CP, are in the Waffen-SS, a Colonel in the medical corps."

"Me, man, what am I supposed to be?" Grinder was patting his pockets. "Is there any money in here, maybe some Reichsmarks, us officers are supposed to have some major coin. What's this hanging from the strap." Grinder was feeling around.

"You're a corporal, and that's a machine gun strapped to you, so don't fuck with it you imbecile." CP said.

"Very good CP, you seem to know your Nazi uniforms, look at the ladies."

"Yeah, look at those broads," grinder said. Nadine's all dolled up like some Kraut groupie, and Milly's got some lab coat and mean looking specs, hair in a bun. This is cool. We look like a landing party from Star Trek."

"Shut up Grinder," Milly said.

"Yes, please do," Beaufort said. "We're escorting this 'prisoner' to the Olympic Village."

"Why you do dat?" Nell said. She was looking at the striped pajama outfit. "I looks like some mofo consecation camp ho."

"That's what you're supposed to look like."

"How're we supposed to pull this off?"

"Just do as I say, and Jesse Owens will never put those inserts in his shoes."

At the moment Herr General Beaufort finished speaking a burst of gunfire followed the three pings of dust floating up from their path.

"Where the hell do you think you're going?"

"Duss?"

"That's right," he was holding a machine gun, one hand holding down the short muzzle so the next burst wouldn't send the bullets flying to high."

"Now now, Herman, you don't need to do this. He'll win without them," Beaufort took a step forward.

"Bullshit," Duss said, and wrapped the gun's strap around his wrist, took aim, and smiled. "You'll die here."

"That would change history forever, Duss. You'll never be born."

"What are you saying?"

"Look over your shoulder," Grinder said.

CP dove at Duss's feet, tackling him. Another burst of machine gun fire.

"Grab him, drag him into the portal."

"You mean I don't get to go have a brew at the Bier Garden?"

"Just drag him into the portal." Milly give him an injection."

"I didn't think it'd be this easy," CP said as they reached the shimmering pane they'd entered 1936 through.

"I did," Beaufort said. "Now we've got to get some answers. After you, CP," Beaufort's jackboot heel disappeared into the vortex of history along with Duss, Nell, and Grinder.

39

INTERVIEW TIME

Doc Beaufort in his "dungeon" with Milly, CP, Grinder, Nell, and Duss tied to a chair.

"Where did you drag me?" Duss muttered.

"Well well well, it's nice to see that you are all together. Different folks from different times with different motivations. And to think Milly and I came here to settle ."

"Why?" Grinder said. "What the fuck're we doin' back here in the friggin' basement?"

"Cellar, Grinder, the cellar." Milly corrected him, and adjusted her peaked nurses's cap.

"Whatever you call it. It looks more like a missile silo," CP said.

"It is." Beaufort added. "We've got Duss here, who's tampered with the space-time continuum by his side trip to 1936. He tried changing the course of history by putting these--he held up the shoe inserts--into Jesse Owens running shoes."

"To slow his ass down," Grinder slapped the time traveling chiropodist tied to the Naugahyde coated, brass rimmed, fake gem encrusted, chiropody chair across his duct taped mouth. "Friggin' douchebag."

Duss squirmed.

"You aren't going anywhere, son." Beaufort added. "You can't change what was, without a ripple in what will be. Fortunately this was considered when we began time travel. Years beyond what your mind would have been capable of considering. In 2050 parts of the human brain were discovered that you couldn't imagine existed. Artists like Dali, Monet, Manet, Duchamp, and de Kooning dreamt of them, even had some fine pictures too. Schizophrenics rambled about alternative realities. Zealots, like Eustice Seeney, attributed that sort of thinking to Heaven and Hell along with millions of earth's great thinkers. It was just an area of the brain which lay asleep, undisturbed, because society's vectors inhibited its function. They had to be crazy, outcasts, loons. No, the human race wasn't ready yet."

"And the extra cyclic nucleotide, mymine, somehow lit up those neurons. And what didn't make sense, became logical sensible ways of viewing the world, right?" CP said.

"Well well well, CP, you're getting ahead of yourself."

"Yeah, CP. What the fuck are you talkin' about?"

"Shut up, Grinder." CP said.

"Very simply, the mymine was as you now know controlled, driven if you will. By pre-programmed systems designed hundreds of years before they were instituted. The mymine became a part of every cell in human bodies implanted with the original chips, and modified to meet the challenges of time paradoxes."

"What the . . . ?" CP said rubbing his forehead.

"I could go for a drink." Grinder added.

"Long before any of us was born, it was anticipated that people would travel back in time, try to manipulate events, use their knowledge, and as we all know that would change things. Of course this was prohibited. But imbeciles like our friend here, the fool who followed you CP, Grinder, and Nadine from 1958 to retrieve the basic elements of mymine from falling into the wrong hands was already pre-programmed. Failure was not an option. Never was. The fact that in 1928 CP, Grinder, Nadine, Milly, and myself were present can never be changed. It occurred. The card game at Cap's place in 1928, between Thomas Edison, Albert Einstein, and Al Capone, for that amber colored gem in my swizzle stick was pre-arranged. The past cannot be changed.

"But this schmuck tried to fuck it up, out of greed," Grinder smacked him again.

"He tried." Nadine said. "I almost never existed."

"That was his plan."

The redneck Seeney, was on to the supercomputers, believing it was some religions construct, and he'll remain so. The computers which now self-replicate are calculating out billions of possibilities by the nanosecond. Making adjustments, and guiding the implanted chips, which by 2070 were already part of naturally occurring DNA," Beaufort sighed.

"So I was born with mymine as part of my DNA all along?" Nadine said.

"Yes. The triplets had at least one mymine that could be activated no matter what would have happened. A rubber band sort of effect. If you travel back in time to change the future, what already was, remains as is. And any attempt to alter it is reconfigured by the machines, to adjust for a harmonic human history."

"No matter what Duss attempted would have failed, right?"

"That's correct, CP."

"However there is a period of transience, where the subtle changes take on a reality that's out of synch with how it's ordained. Poor choice of words, but determined to not do anything that could infringe on the existence of the self-developing, continually evolving geometry of time and space. The evolving computers, which are part human, part machine cannot allow for anything to alter their trajectory. I was part of their development, and remain as a guardian of sorts, of history's continuity. I know I know, it can all seem so mind boggling, but let's activate some cortex, and it'll all be much more clear." Beaufort waved an open palm. There was a static in the air, and a hum, the lights dimmed, and then the atmosphere changed, followed by an audible pop.

"Bibbidi friggin' Bobbidi friggin' Boo." Grinder said, reaching for a cigarette.

"No smoking Grinder," Milly said.

"I was just . . . Mother fucker, I get it."

"Get what Grinder?"

"Motherfucker, man. We're all meant to be here, everything's that happened had to happen. Shit."

"What" Some light bulb went on up in your haid, cracker?" Nell said.

At that, Duss's tape had torn. His head increased by five sizes, and he was out of the chiropody chair. He grabbed Milly by the throat and began to squeeze.

"I'll kill her, I swear it I'll kill her if you don't do as I say."

"What's that?" Beaufort said.

"Open a portal, send me back to 1977."

CP started to move toward him.

Duss squoze harder. "I'll kill the bitch if you do anything."

At that, Beaufort took an ancient hypodermic syringe from his pocket, lunged at Duss, and pressed the plunger.

He was out.

"I don't think that some folks should have any memory of this at all. No no no. Does anyone else think so?"

"Hey you're the history buff," Grinder said.

"Good."

The room went dark.

"What happened?" CP said.

"Duss wasn't born with mymine chips. He had ordinary cyclic nucleotides, and wasn't built to evolve. He'll simply awake with no memory of anything but his own experience. He'll be back shaving corns in an hour."

"And that's it?" CP said.

"Well, you, Nadine, Grinder, Nell, are here, in 1958. That can't remain as is. Two humans are going to return to 2013. CP and Nadine. I cannot alter what you know, but you know it. I can only tell you what knowledge you have will be the stuff of science fiction in 2013, that's where you belong. I cannot alter that."

"I'm not sure what you mean?" CP said.

Beaufort continued: "What you're imaginations do, is up to you. Nadine, you're presence in 2013 is imperative, you're pregnant. The child will grow up to develop the first of many steps along the way to ensure my existence. If I did not help you return to the past, I would cease to exist. The fact that I am here, now, is testament to the fact that this is true."

As soon as he spoke the final words, a shimmering wall of glass appeared, and one by one, they stepped through it.

Grinder, you and Nell will remain here. Those two thugs, Alejandro and Bart Pinto? Their death or disappearance in 2013 won't be missed, but two bodies will reappear--two souls--if you will. That will set the grand scheme of things. So here is where you'll remain. I can't change that.

Grinder looked at Nell. " I can dig that," sizing her up.

"What you lookin' at fool. You be the first cracker be wit a colored gal, you best be treatin' my black ass right. I gonna dig it back here."

40

1977

"All right all right, I'm comin'," the woman shouted from the kitchen of her third floor condominium in Boca Raton, Florida. Company? She stopped slicing onions, rinsed her hands, and turned down the volume of the stereo. Fercockta disco music. Who comes to visit at this time of day? She mumbled to herself as she left the counter where she was slicing onions for an egg salad sandwich. The King had died, and she was a wreck. The stench wafted their sulphur laden odors through the quaint one bedroom one bath unit. Her eyes were moist because she'd been crying. Elvis died yesterday. Who the hell shows up at this time of day. It was two PM, and the summer sun was glaring through her sliding glass door which faced the south west. She yelled out: "Hang on, I gotta get the phone," and took a couple steps to where it sat on the kitchen table, picked up the handpiece, and said, "Hang on someone's at the door," without letting them reply. She would have drawn the blinds, the damn air conditioning bill was ridiculous, but hurried over to the door. Maybe it's a repairman she thought. Damn thing was making funny noises, maybe the condo association finally got someone to look at these things. Eh, she thought, you never know. "I'm coming," the woman said.

She put her left eye up to the peep hole, and stared out. There was no one there. She pivoted, went back to the phone, and said: "That was strange, I swear somebody knocked on my door, but nobody was there. Eh, condos. I'm making a nice sandwich for you."

He ate the onion laced egg salad sandwich, at his aunt's condominium and drove back to the University of Miami Medical School. The girl in his study group was waiting at the library, the one he fancied. Looking at her classmate she shook her head, then looked at her watch, and said: "What kept you?"

"I had to meet my aunt for lunch," he moved his face close and whispered. "Who's your friend?"

"I'm late for class already, you need some mints," she said.

She looked at her friend, rolled her eyes, and said: "You can go over biochemistry with him. I've got to go. His breath is horrible," she gathered her books to leave. "I have to get going. You two can go over the this without me." She glanced at the library table with books and papers covering it's top. She would later recall that his breath was so foul her eyes watered. Her friend, another twenty-four year old girl, stood up, went over to the gal on her way out, and said: "He's cute," and proceeded to give him a breath mint. They had sex in the stacks between bookshelves on the second floor. Nine months later she gave birth to a baby girl. Twenty eight years later her daughter gave birth to another girl. Years later, her granddaughter gave birth to another child, and named her Nadine.

So much for onion sandwiches.